MW00877495

# STORM
# WALKER

ALSO BY MIKE REVELL

*Stonebird*

# STORM WALKER

# WALKER

## MIKE REVELL

Quercus

New York • London

# Quercus

ISBN 978-1-68144-493-2

Library of Congress Cataloging in Publication Control Number: 2016032771

Distributed in the United States and Canada by
Hachette Book Group
1290 Avenue of the Americas
New York, NY 10104

Manufactured in the United States

10 9 8 7 6 5 4 3 2 1

www.quercus.com

*For my parents, who have always
believed in the magic of stories*

# 1

I blame it on the nosebleed.

If I hadn't gone to the nurse's office I never would have seen the leaflets, and Dad would never have gone to counseling, and my life wouldn't have taken a turn for the crazy. Trust me, if I had the choice between living like a normal twelve-year-old and jumping into a dead world, I'd grab normal every time.

But I had to take the header. It was the National School Football Championships—if we lost the game, we'd be knocked out, and I'd never get trials for Cambridge. And that meant sprinting back to the box with the rest of the lads and trying to clear Shepworth's corner.

"Get it out!" Mr. Matthews yelled. "Whatever you do, just get it out!"

I glanced at Danny, nodding in the direction of their goal. If we managed to clear it, I'd thread it through to him and we'd be able to break.

Danny grinned. He knew exactly what I was thinking.

The ref blew the whistle and the ball looped in. It curved in slow motion, and as I leapt up I saw water droplets spraying off it in every direction. I wasn't a great defender but could head it pretty well, and all I had to do was clear it, just like Mr. Matthews said.

But as I jumped, something caught my eye, and I turned—

*CRUNCH.*

The ball smashed into my nose and I stumbled over, shielding myself from the rush of cleats.

"Clear it!" someone barked.

"Boot it away!"

When I took my hands from my face, they were covered in blood.

The whistle blew and at first I thought they'd scored. I looked up, but everyone had stopped and the ref was jogging over to me, waving at our sideline.

"Are you all right?" he said. "Look at me. How many fingers am I holding up?"

I swiped at sweat and tears and tried to focus. "Three," I said.

Mr. Matthews knelt beside me and soaked the magic sponge in water, sloshing it all over my face as he dabbed at my nose. It wasn't really a magic sponge, it was just called that because if you got smacked in the shin it really did take away the pain.

"What were you thinking?" he said.

"I was trying to get rid of it. I was trying to smash it out of the box."

"I know you were, son. Now put your head back."

He pinched my nose and held the sponge under it, but I could feel the blood still gushing out. Sweat stung my eyes now and I scrunched them tight shut. The referee moved closer and muttered something in Mr. Matthews's ear.

"We're going to have to move you," he said. "Reckon you can stand up?"

I pushed myself off the ground, but as I did I caught sight of the sponge. Normally I'm all right with gory stuff. Last week in Science we cut open an eyeball and Sarah Bromley and Zach Goodman had to leave the room because it made them feel sick. That didn't bother me at all.

But the sponge . . .

It was red—deep red—and dripping. I tasted warm blood on my lips and before I could take a step, everything went gray and fizzy, like when you load up a bad channel on TV. The last thing I heard was my name, over and over again.

"Owen. Owen?"

I slumped to the ground.


"Owen!"

That voice. I recognized that voice. I blinked and tried to sit up, but my head pounded. "What happened?" I asked, squinting up at Danny.

"You just proved why you don't play defense," he said.

My hand shot to my nose and I winced as I felt for damage, but when I looked at my fingers, there was no blood. The door creaked open, and the school nurse shuffled into the room. "Lucky it's not broken," she said. "Idiot boys and your idiot games. Why you'd want to go chasing a ball around a field is beyond me."

But her lips twitched, and I knew she wasn't being mean.

The clock on the wall said 5:01. I must have only been out for a few seconds, but what a time to black out—I'd missed the end of the game! An ice-cold feeling rippled through my stomach as I thought back to the end of the match. I hardly dared ask the question . . . but in the end I didn't need to. Danny saw my face and answered for me.

"We won," he said. "Just."

Yes! We had made it through! Two more wins and we'd be in the quarter final.

If we got that far, there would be scouts for sure. Academy scouts at our game . . .

"What happened?" Danny said, snapping me out of the dream. "At the end of the match? I've never seen you miss a ball like that before."

"I . . . I don't know," I said. Which was a lie.

Because I did know. I took my eye off the ball at the last second, not because I was nervous, but because I saw her. I saw Mum. Except I didn't. I couldn't have.

Three hundred and fifty-five days. That was how long it'd been since they buried her. Every time I closed my eyes, I could feel the cold rain on my skin. Dad holding me under the too-small umbrella while the vicar went on and on about how amazing she was. Saying Cambridge had lost a cherished member of the community.

But the people in town didn't know her. Not really. They hadn't played Monopoly with her or watched her fail at Just Dance or seen her make smiley faces with the mushy peas when we got fish and chips. All they saw were her paintings.

"Are you all right, mate?" Danny said.

I shook the thoughts away. "Yeah. Yeah, I'm fine."

Which was another lie.

One more sleep. That was all it was. Tomorrow, it would be a year since the Longest Day. How could I be fine when the anniversary was coming up?

I grabbed some leaflets off a table and pretended to flick through them, but really I was just trying to clear my head.

"You can go home," the nurse said. "Just don't go smacking yourself in the face for a while."

I looked at Danny. He beamed, bouncing up and down on his toes, then skipped out of the office. I gathered my things, which had been dumped in the corner of the room, and followed him out of school.

The buses were all gone now, so we walked home, kicking a football all the way. I smiled and laughed along with

Danny's jokes, but I couldn't stop my mind drifting. I know it wasn't Mum at the game. There was no one there. It was all in my imagination. But she had seemed so real.

And if *I* was cracking up like this, how much worse was it for Dad?

# 2

When I got in I went straight up to my room, chucked my stuff on the floor, and changed out of my football gear. It was only then that I noticed the leaflets, falling out of my bag. I must have stuffed them in there without thinking back in the nurse's office.

One had a photo of a chalky-faced kid on the front. His eyes had dark circles underneath them and he looked as if he was about to throw up. The heading across the top read JUST SAY NO in big red letters.

I scrunched it up, and was just about to get rid of the others too when something made me stop. The photo on the front of the second one . . .

It wasn't anything to do with drugs. There were gravestones, and people hugging or standing with their heads bowed low. The title said WE ARE ALWAYS HERE TO HELP.

I scanned the text inside, looking for something in it that might help Dad. It had a load of words on it like "Depression and Anxiety" and "Anger and Loss," but it didn't go into any detail. Further down, it listed the different types of counseling available—things like "Artistic Healing" and "Musical Medicine." Then it just had a load of pictures, and a quote from a girl who ran away from home and found help through counseling.

But I didn't want to run away from home. I just wanted Dad to be okay.

Ever since the Longest Day, he'd been getting quieter. He never came to watch me play anymore, and he stopped asking to kick the ball around with me months ago. It could be annoying but I couldn't get mad, because even though the Longest Day had been awful for me, it must have been worse for him. I'd only known Mum for eleven years, and some of that I was a baby, so for those years I didn't really know her at all. But Dad was married to her for fifteen. He had lived with her every day, and now she'd gone.

I looked again at that term—"Artistic Healing." Dad was an author, but he hadn't written anything in over a year. Back when he *did* write, he used to sit in his study for hours and when he emerged, there was a spring in his step. Maybe these people could get him writing again?

Right at the bottom of the leaflet, there was a number to ring. I hesitated, wondering whether I should call, wondering what would happen if I did. Maybe I could just leave the leaflet on his bedside cabinet? No, he'd know right away it was me. I could call the counselors myself . . . get them to talk to Dad, without him knowing it was me.

I stared at the leaflet, memories of Mum's funeral racing through my head, until something jolted me out of my thoughts.

The fire alarm.

Still holding the leaflet in my hand, I rushed downstairs. Smoke filled the hall in a gray haze. It wasn't thick, but it smelled rank, and I covered my nose with my T-shirt as I stumbled into the kitchen.

"Dad!" I blurted, smoke stinging my eyes.

"It's all right!" he said, flapping a tea towel uselessly at the fire alarm on the ceiling. "I've got everything under control."

I glanced round, trying not to breathe in. There was a pan on the stove with what looked like thick black treacle glued to it.

"What's that?" I moved closer.

"It was going to be dinner," Dad said. "But since this is what happens when you try to crack into it, it's not anymore." He held something up, but my eyes were watering so much I had to rub them dry before I could make out what it was.

What it used to be, anyway. Now the spoon looked more like the metal pegs used to pin tents down with. It was curved in three places, bent completely out of shape.

"Are these beans?" I said, turning back to what used to be dinner.

When Dad said he was cooking dinner, what he really meant was he was throwing a ready meal in the oven or pouring something out of a can. He used to be a great cook. Before the Longest Day, he'd done most of the cooking, shutting himself in the kitchen while he worked on hand-pressed burgers or homemade pizza. But ever since then, it was as if something had squashed all the interest out of him. You didn't get meals like this if you loved cooking.

"Er, yes," he said.

"I didn't think it was possible to burn beans."

He chuckled. "Well, you learn something new every day."

He sloshed water into the sink and threw the pan in with a squeeze of dish soap. The smell of lemon balm filled the kitchen—it was Mum's favorite smell, lemony and minty at the same time, and Dad kept buying it.

"How about we get takeout, eh?" Dad said, rubbing his face. Before the Longest Day he used to shave all the time, but now his cheeks were always covered in gray stubble. "Your choice. Whatever you like."

We ordered pizza from the new restaurant in town and sat in front of the TV with the greasy boxes. Dad flicked through the channels, settling on a repeat of *Top Gear*. But even though pizza was the Food of Kings, and even though Danny once bet me I'd never be able to eat a whole large one to myself and I did and he paid me ten pounds, today my stomach clenched at the sight of it. I took a bite, but the more I chewed, the less hungry I got.

"Get it down you," Dad said. "You could do with putting on a few pounds."

I took another bite and felt Dad's eyes on me as I gulped it down. I locked my gaze on the TV and tried to fight off the image of Mum at the football game, but I couldn't.

"I saw her," I said. I didn't really want to tell him, because he had enough on his plate and I didn't want him worrying about me. But the lemon balm had brought it all back, and I couldn't keep it in anymore.

"Saw who?" Dad said, but as soon as the words left his mouth, he knew. "Oh . . ."

His face clouded over, and he turned to look out of the window. In the first few weeks after the Longest Day, Dad looked out of the window a lot. I don't just mean little glances. He'd look out for ten minutes at a time, just staring and staring into the distance.

Sometimes he'd do it in the middle of conversations. He'd be saying something like, "Then I just . . ." And he'd sigh quietly, and stop, like he didn't even know he was doing it. At first I thought it was because of his writing. Mum always said he walked around with half his mind on his stories. Dad used to laugh when she said that. *Never been much of a talker,* he'd say. *Maybe that's why I became a writer in the first place.*

But this was different. The pauses lasted longer, and whenever he blinked them away I could tell he wasn't thinking about stories at all.

He turned back to me now, his lips pulled tight. "I see her all the time," he said gently. "I saw her earlier, when I was cooking dinner. She was right there in the kitchen with me. Next thing I knew, the fire alarm was going off."

I didn't know what to say. My mouth hung open uselessly. He was giving me that look again, the same look he had when my hamster, Spotty, died and he didn't know how to tell me. It felt good to talk about seeing Mum, but part of me burned with shame for bringing it up. That was the first time I'd ever seen her so clearly like that, and it was probably just because the anniversary was coming up. But Dad just said he saw her all the time. At least I had football to take my mind off it. Dad . . . since he stopped writing, he had nothing.

"It's completely normal," Dad said finally.

"Yeah," I said, jarred from my thoughts.

Dad shuffled closer. "Did you think you were going mad?"

"I . . . I don't know. A bit, maybe."

I never should have brought it up. It didn't matter how I felt.

"Well, you're not." Dad was quiet for a moment, maybe picking his words carefully. "Owen, you've been through something that no one should have to go through. We both have. It's normal for us to think about her. That's all it is. Just thoughts."

My eyes moved to the urn on the mantelpiece. The light from the TV flashed against it, turning it blue-gold.

"We'll do it," Dad said, following my gaze. He meant chucking Mum's ashes out to sea. That was what she wanted us to do. It was in her will. Dad took a deep breath, and it shuddered on the way out. "We'll do it. Just not yet, eh? Not yet."

"Yeah," I said. He'd been talking about scattering Mum's ashes for months. Once I actually thought we were going to do it. We were sitting in the car, strapped in, ready to go, but as soon as the engine grumbled into life, Dad went back on the plan.

I wanted to say something to help now, but was scared of getting it wrong.

I shoved my hands in my pockets, and felt something inside them. The leaflet. Maybe if I could get Dad some help, he'd be there to cheer us on in the next round of the championships. Maybe he'd go back to cooking his usual meals instead of getting takeout every day. Maybe we really would throw Mum's ashes out to sea.

I took the leaflet out—

"What have you got there?" Dad said. His eyes moved over the title, and suddenly he put his plate on the table and took the leaflet from my hands. "Owen . . . who gave you this? Is everything okay?" His eyes were lined with worry. "If there's anything on your mind, you can talk to me. I know I haven't exactly been brilliant recently, but I'll . . . I'll always be here. I want to help."

"It's okay," I said, forcing a smile to let him know I was all right. "I don't even know why I've still got it. But I thought it might be good for . . . for you."

I looked away as soon as I said it, because the expression on Dad's face changed from concern to shock, then something else. Something I hadn't seen before.

"You think I need counseling?" he said.

"I just thought . . ."

But how could I say it? *I just thought it might bring my old dad back.* I stared at my hands, wishing I'd never brought the stupid leaflet back from the nurse's office in the first place.

"Did your teacher give this to you? What's she been saying? I know I've been a bit disconnected—God knows I do—but it'll pass, Owen. I just need a bit of time."

"I'm just trying to help," I said, turning to face him again.

He'd already had time. We both had. After Mum died I had a week off school, and I felt like I never wanted to go again. But I had to. I could still remember the day I'd gone back in. Mrs. Willoughby pulled the Sad Face when she saw me. The whole class stopped talking. Their eyes followed me all the way to my desk. Everyone knew about Mum's death. It was in the papers and everything. I guessed when a local artist died it was big news. I knew everyone was trying to make sure they didn't upset me, but all I wanted to do was forget about it, and they just made it worse by acting so weird.

The one thing I learned was that you could never get over it. Not really. You just had to keep living your life, and eventually better memories would rise up to balance out the bad ones. But Dad . . . he didn't keep going. He stopped. It was like he was sinking in quicksand.

"I'm not getting counseling, Owen," he said. Then he reached out and shook my shoulder gently. "I'm all right. I promise."

"Fine," I said, my cheeks burning.

I didn't feel like talking after that so left my pizza unfinished and went back upstairs to play some FIFA football. The game was just loading up when I heard the outside door bang shut. I walked over to the window and saw Dad's dark silhouette moving in the garden.

Normally Dad stood tall, his shoulders pulled back like a robot doing an impression of a human. But sometimes, if he didn't know I could see him, like now, he slouched as if an invisible weight was hanging off his shoulders and it was too much for him to take.

My stomach twisted. What was he up to? He loved gardening, but it was too dark for that now. He moved out of sight and, hesitating for just a second, I rushed across the landing to the bathroom window. I squinted through the gloom, trying to spot him again. Then three yellow squares lit up at the end of the garden and Dad's silhouette appeared, hunched over in the middle of the shed. Mum's shed.

I hadn't been in there since the Longest Day. I didn't think Dad had either, but I must've got that wrong, because he didn't pause before he went inside, like I would have done. He walked straight in.

I closed my eyes and tried to remember what the paintings looked like. All the work Mum had started and not finished, or the stuff she didn't want to sell. But I hadn't seen them for so long that the memories were hazy. I couldn't imagine them properly. It was like when you went on vacation and had an amazing time but a few years later you couldn't remember what you did, just the feeling it gave you afterward.

I opened my eyes. Dad hadn't moved. I watched for another minute, wondering what he was doing, then decided to give him some privacy. Maybe he was seeing Mum again, like I'd seen her at the game. I went back to my room and played FIFA until my eyelids got heavy.

I only realized I'd fallen asleep when I heard the scream.

# 3

I blinked and shook my head, trying to wake up. My cheek ached from where it had been pressed up against the Play-Station controller.

How long had I been asleep for?

I thought back to Dad, outside in the shed yesterday evening, and that was when it hit me. My heart beat faster, and I couldn't tell if it was from the shock of the scream or the realization. Today was the anniversary. A year since the Longest Day.

I scrambled off the bed and crept across the landing, trying not to make a sound. It was a bit strange he hadn't checked in on me last night. Even after Mum died, he usually opened the door to say goodnight and make sure that I was okay. It didn't bother me that he hadn't . . . I mean, I was twelve years old, not a baby. What bothered me was that since the Longest Day, Dad had been so off—and now it looked like he was getting worse. I wished he would see someone about it, *do* something about it, just to see if it could help.

"Dad?" I whispered. The scream had come from his room, I was sure of it now.

I pushed the door open a crack. He was mumbling to himself. Whispering in his sleep.

I crept into the room. I didn't know why, but I was holding my breath. The place was a mess. Dirty clothes all over the floor, magazines and dusty books piled up in the corner. All the photos on the bedside table had been flipped over, so you couldn't see them.

All apart from one—the one in Dad's hands. He must have fallen asleep looking at it.

"Dad."

He blinked slowly, and opened his eyes.

"Owen?" he said. "What are you doing?"

"You screamed."

"I . . . I did?"

He sighed heavily, rubbing the sleep from his eyes. He frowned at the photo, as if it had walked onto the bed while he was asleep. Then he sat up and put the frame facedown on the bedside table.

In the low morning light, I could almost imagine the shape of Mum's body outlined in the wrinkles of the sheet beside Dad. He patted the duvet. "It's okay," he said.

I took a deep breath, and lay down next to him. He drew me in next to his warm chest. The silence stretched.

All I could hear was the low rattle and hum of the heating as the pipes came to life. I didn't know what to say. We hadn't spoken since he took the leaflet, and part of me was still angry at him, so I sat there in silence waiting for Dad to talk.

"Maybe you were right," he said finally.

"W-what?" I croaked, clearing my throat and licking my dry lips.

He looked at me, chewing the words round in his mouth. "Maybe you were right. Look at me. I'm a mess!" And suddenly he burst out laughing, although it wasn't a proper laugh, the kind where you couldn't help but join in because it was so infectious. It was a different kind of laugh. A scary laugh.

"My own son," Dad spluttered. "Better father than I am."

My fingers knotted together automatically. I didn't know what to do.

"I . . . I'm sorry," I said.

"Don't be! You've got nothing to be sorry for. You were only trying to help. I'm lucky to have you looking out for me. My very own guardian angel."

I didn't know what to say to that, so I just kept quiet, listening to the house and the sounds of the birds waking up outside.

"'Artistic Healing,'" he scoffed. "Well, it can't hurt to go along. You never know, they might get me writing again. Got to get it out somehow, eh?"

"I guess," I said, shuffling up beside him and grinning.

Counseling! He was actually going to go. After all that.

Hearing him say it out loud made all the worries building up inside me melt away. I'd been dreading going to school today. I couldn't stop worrying that it would be exactly the same as the week after Mum died. The long silences. The Sad Face. The awkwardness. But if Dad could go to counseling, then I could go to school. I knew that much.

Dad squeezed me tight, and I smiled up at him, happy just to lie in silence for the last few minutes before I had to get ready.


You could hear the noise all the way down the corridor— laughing, shouting. When I opened the door, I only just dodged a rubber band pinging across the room. Some of the tables were upturned. People ducked behind them, in the middle of a war.

For a heartbeat, nobody moved.

I stood in the doorway as the sudden quiet washed over me.

*This is it,* I told myself, trying to pretend it wasn't quiet, trying to reimagine the noise from a few moments earlier. *They're going to act all weird again, just like they did after Mum died.*

But then, in a flurry of movement, the war continued. Rubber bands pinged. Fresh shouts took up, ringing around the class. They must have worried that it was Mrs. Willoughby at the door, because as soon as they saw it was me, they went back to normal. They didn't know it was the anniversary at all. None of them did. Not even Danny.

I walked into the room, alone in my own personal quiet. I could still hear the sound of the play-fight around me, but it was distant—like when you're zoning out before you fall asleep, and the sound of the TV becomes white noise.

Of course they wouldn't remember. It was just a normal day to them, wasn't it? They didn't have it hanging over them, plodding closer and closer. I bet their dads didn't wake up screaming in the middle of the night.

I hardly noticed the door open again, but it must have been Mrs. Willoughby coming in because all of a sudden clattering and banging filled the room as the class shoved the desks back into place. I turned to the window, watching a potato chip bag dancing in the wind. The clouds were darkening. Rain speckled the glass. I tried not to think of Mum, but it was really hard not to think of something when you were trying to avoid it.

"Earth to Owen," Danny said, waving his hands in front of me.

"S-sorry," I mumbled. He'd sat down beside me and was staring at my face as if he couldn't believe what he was seeing.

"How can you not be more excited? They've put the schedule up!"

I blinked at him, trying to figure out what he meant. His phone was open on the football league page, which showed a table of all the upcoming games. The game . . . it had tumbled right out of my mind. Something must have clicked when Danny saw my face, because next thing I knew his smile faded. His eyebrows shot up and his forehead wrinkled. He froze, no longer bursting with excitement.

"Oh crap," he said. "It's—"

"Don't worry," I said quickly. "I'm trying not to think about it."

I took the phone from his hand and zoomed in on our match.

"Westfield," I read. "Where are they from?"

"Er—somewhere near Leicester," Danny mumbled. He cleared his throat. "They've got a goal difference of plus thirteen too."

"They haven't played us yet, though, have they?" I said, trying to sound upbeat.

Danny smiled hesitantly, and smacked me playfully on the arm. "If we beat them, the scouts will have to come. It's up to us, mate. Ronaldo and Messi," he said, lips twitching as if he was holding back a bigger grin.

"Thor and Iron Man," I said.

"Arthur and Lancelot," Danny shot back.

"Batman and—"

"You better not be calling me Robin," he said.

I couldn't help laughing. It was such a stupid game, but it always made me smile. And the best thing about it was that, for a while at least, it took my mind right off the Longest Day.

The anniversary started so well, with Dad finally going to counseling and Danny making me laugh, that I should have known it would never last. When I got home after school, I couldn't find Dad anywhere. The weather was worse now. Rain lashed the windows, and the wind whistled as it whipped through the trees. I looked for Dad all through the house—even in the study, in case he'd been in there, but he was nowhere to be seen.

"Dad?" I called, each breath coming faster now.

Then I remembered last night, and ran outside into the rain. Covering my face with the collar of my school jacket, I dashed round to the back garden. Dad always said Mum's artist studio should stay how she left it forever. But now the lights were on, illuminating the end of the garden. He was in there again. The second night in a row.

*What's he doing?*

I crept closer, holding my breath. The grass squelched underfoot. The wind howled. When I got closer, I could see Dad through the nearest window. He had his back to me and his arms wrapped round his tummy, like he was doing that trick where you turned your back to someone and hugged yourself, and if you wriggled your arms the right way it looked like you were kissing someone.

But he wasn't kissing someone. I knew that much. I approached the doorway and stood there quietly. His shoulders shook, up and down, up and down.

"Dad?" I said.

He jumped and spun around, making a big O with his mouth. "Owen. It's only you. You've got me jumping at ghosts."

"I didn't mean to surprise you," I said, noticing the tears in his eyes. "I was just wondering what you were doing out here."

His gaze was already drifting back to the paintings. They lined the walls of the shed. Most of them were animals or landscapes, but some were more abstract. I used to love watching Mum paint, and seeing how messy she made it. She didn't just brush the paint on. She forced it on like she was attacking the canvas. There were huge dry splodges all over them. You could run your hand down one and it would feel 3-D.

"I've been coming here more and more since . . . you know."

He still couldn't bring himself to say it. *Since Mum died.* They were just words. But I guessed sometimes words could be scary. Mum was dead. It was easy to think it, but much harder to say it. It weighed down your tongue and filled your mind with horrible images that weren't nice to think about.

Death was a scary word. But the L-word was the scariest. I didn't like saying that. It made my stomach churn and my mind explode in a million different directions. It was easier to pretend it didn't exist.

"They're brilliant," Dad said. "The paintings. They're really good."

"Yeah," I said.

Silence fell between us. Talking was hard when there were so many things you couldn't say even when you were thinking about them. I knew what I could say. What I should say.

*I love you.*

The words were there, but they didn't come out. Not because I didn't love him. I did, loads and loads. With Mum I could say it all the time and it wouldn't feel strange. But with Dad . . . it just didn't feel right. I was worried that if I said it, I might sound babyish. And I wanted Dad to know that I was grown up.

I wanted to help him, but I didn't know how. That was why the counseling was so important. They were trained for things like this, weren't they? They'd know what to do. Except . . . it couldn't have worked, because Dad was worse than ever.

"Did you go?" I said, a sudden thought occurring to me.

"What?"

"Did you go to counseling?"

"Owen, not this again . . ."

"You said you'd go. You promised."

There was a crack of thunder outside the shed. The light flickered, throwing us into shadow, then flashed back into life. Dad was staring at me, his hands on his hips.

"I know what I said. But I think it's probably best if I don't go. It's . . . awkward, Owen. I don't want anyone digging into our life. I'll be all right."

"But you're not all right, are you?" I said, surprising myself with how loud my voice was. The wind slammed into the shed and I thought the light would go out again, but it didn't. "You haven't been to see me play in over a year. You've stopped asking how I'm doing when I get home from school. You always make excuses not to go out, like with parents' evening at school. Mrs. Willoughby's never even met you!"

"Owen—"

"You don't care about cooking anymore. We just have takeout all the time. I hate it! And I can't even remember the last time you wrote anything!"

"Owen, listen to me—"

"You said you'd go!" I shouted, trying to make myself heard above the storm. "They had Artistic Healing and everything. You probably wouldn't even *have* to talk. You could just write. You used to love writing. It was all you ever wanted to do, and now—now you don't do anything!"

"Will you be quiet?" Dad yelled, and the silence that followed was smashed by the roar of the wind and the constant pouring rain. "I can't write. Not anymore. It's ... it's too hard."

"You can't just stop," I said, getting quieter now. The sudden surge of anger was fading, and in its place was just emptiness. Why couldn't he see? If he just *tried*, maybe he'd feel better. Writing always made him feel better.

Dad didn't say anything to that. He just stood there, his hands on his hips. Behind him, through torrents of rain rippling down the window, the storm raged on. Lightning flashed, illuminating his face—so pale, so tired.

"Fine," he said, marching past me to the door. "You want me to write? I'll write. I'll go into that study right now and *bleed* onto that page if I have to. Will that make you happy?"

He turned and shoved the door, striding out into the lashing rain. The door banged on its hinges, then swung back hard, thumping against the wooden frame. Lightning forked again, sparking across the sky.

I was balling my fists so hard my nails dug into the skin. I rubbed my palms to get rid of the pain. My knees shook and shook. I'd never argued with Dad before, not properly. Part of me wanted to run out and apologize already, but I couldn't. Why couldn't he have just gone to counseling like he'd said?

I took a deep breath, trying to calm myself down. I stood there staring at the paintings and the minutes stretched until I lost track of time. My Art teacher, Mrs. Bridges, was always saying we should look for the meaning in paintings. Apparently every detail could be important, from the angle to the colors. I didn't know what the message was in Mum's paintings. Maybe she was just trying to show that the world could be a beautiful place.

That was what I was thinking when it happened.

My stomach lurched.

Back in primary school, we used to go over a bumpy bridge in our minibus every morning. Down the road to the bridge all the kids used to sing, *Faster, faster, faster!* Then when we shot over the bridge, our stomachs soared right up into our throats.

That was how this felt now.

I gripped the work surface with both hands, taking deep breaths to steady myself. My heart beat faster and faster, as if I'd just scored a goal.

Then I looked up and blinked in shock.

It was so dark outside now that the light from the shed turned the window into a mirror. Mum's paintings reflected back at me. I could see myself clearly.

Except . . .

No, I must have been imagining it.

Even though it was me in the reflection . . . even though when I moved my hands, the hands in the reflection moved too . . . even though I could see that it was me, I also knew that it wasn't.

It wasn't me.

I moved closer, squinting at my face. My hair was blond. It was supposed to be dark and scruffy, but now it looked as if I'd dyed it. And my nose . . . it was always big, but it wasn't *that* big. I held up my hands, hardly daring to breathe. My fingers trembled as I felt round my face, exploring the features. I closed my eyes and counted to three, but when I opened them again, the not-me was still there.

"No way," I whispered, the words getting lost in a distant boom of thunder.

I backed away from the window, panic fluttering inside me. People's faces didn't just change. Maybe it was a trick of the light. That could be it.

In a mad rush, I threw open the door of the shed, making sure to shut it behind me so none of the paintings got ruined in the storm. Then I legged it inside, up the stairs, and into the bathroom. If I could just get a proper look at my face . . .

*No* . . .

I gulped, trying to wet the back of my dry throat. Because now I could see it clearly, and it was worse than I'd thought. It wasn't me. My face belonged to someone else entirely.

# 4

It took me ages to get to sleep that night. I kept opening the camera on my phone and pressing the reverse lens so I could check my face. But every time I looked, it wasn't me staring back.

I took a photo, just to have proof it was happening. I zoomed in, a sick feeling squirming in my stomach, creeping slowly up to my throat. Clenching my teeth to hold it back, I chucked my phone onto the bedside table, trying to force it out of my mind.

Dad's footsteps creaked on the stairs. I heard him shuffling up to the door. It opened a crack, and a shaft of light pierced the shadows.

I wanted to talk to him. I wanted to show him what was happening to me. But I still felt embarrassed after the argument, so I curled up to hide my face. I held my breath, pretending to be asleep.

"Goodnight, Owen," Dad whispered.

Then he closed the door.

He'd checked in on me, even after we shouted at each other. A pang of guilt stabbed at me for bringing it up earlier. It wasn't like I *needed* him to do it, but it was nice that he did.

I rolled over, breathing hard. I forced myself to forget about my face. I had to be imagining it. The stress of everything lately, it was obviously getting to me.

I tried counting sheep, but every time I got to ten they disappeared and my new face swam into view. If I kept on like this, I'd never get to sleep. And I needed to stay as sharp as possible if I wanted to help the lads beat Westfield next week.

I forgot about the sheep, and imagined myself into the game. I was putting the ball on the turf, ready to take a free kick. The ref blasted his whistle, trying to tell the Westfield boys to get back. Out of the corner of my eye, I could see Mr. Matthews pacing up and down the sideline, chewing on gum.

If I scored this, we'd win the game . . .


The next thing I knew the alarm was bleeping, flashing insistently that it was time to get up for school. For a second I lay there blinking.

Did I score the free kick? Or did the other team manage to—

The memory of last night slammed into me. I scrambled for my phone, held up the camera.

I couldn't believe it . . .

The blond hair, the thick eyebrows, the way-too-big nose. It was all gone. I was back to being me again. Back to plain old Owen Smith.

I sank into the pillow, letting relief wash over me.

Then I remembered the photo. I must have imagined that too. Right? I sat up, breathing fast, hoping desperately that it had all been in my head. My thumb hesitated over the little gallery icon in the corner of the phone. Bracing myself, I pressed it and the most recent photo flicked up . . .

And there it was.

The blond hair.

The too-big nose.

The features that weren't mine.

The bottom of my stomach dropped away, leaving nothing but a gaping hole. Mr. Herring was always saying the brain was a marvelous thing . . . but you couldn't take photos of stuff you were imagining, could you?

Somehow, it must have really happened. But that was ridiculous. It was impossible.

*It's okay,* I told myself, even though it was hard to believe it. For now, at least, I was back to being me. It wasn't enough to soothe my nerves completely, but it was something. I took a long, slow breath to calm myself down. I deleted the photo to help me forget about it.

If it happened again, *then* I'd worry.

Dad was still asleep, so to keep my mind busy I went downstairs and put the kettle on. I slotted two pieces of bread into the toaster and poured him a glass of orange juice. Then I grabbed a bowl and made myself some cereal.

"Dad!" I called, after a while. "Breakfast."

I flicked the TV on, but there was nothing good on— just the news. This woman was going on about a parrot that could do math, tapping its foot to count out the answers. Some of the sums it could work out faster than me.

"All right?" Dad said, sliding onto the chair closest to the door. He gulped some orange juice, and his eyes latched onto me. He hadn't shaved for days now, and the silvery hairs on his cheeks made him look like an old wolf. "You look—"

"I look what?" I said quickly, touching my cheek self-consciously.

But I was still me. I was still normal.

"You look tired." Dad frowned. His eyes drifted over my face, and it felt as though he was seeing those other features even though they weren't there. "Look, Owen, about yesterday—"

"It's okay," I said.

"No, it's not. You were right. You've been right all along. I think I will go to see those counselors, for real this time. Writing last night, it felt good." He chuckled, as if it surprised him. "It felt really good. The story's not quite there yet, but it's coming."

He didn't have to say anything—I could tell from his laughter. I couldn't remember the last time I'd heard him chuckle like that. And if one writing session made him feel better, imagine how much good it would do him if he kept at it?

"What's it about?" I asked.

"Ah, I can't tell you that. Not yet. Got to give it a chance to brew first. Wouldn't want to jinx it. But I'll tell you what . . . I think you'll like it. The hero's a lot like you."

# 5

By the time I got to school, the shock of the evening before had faded. I tried googling it and I reckoned I'd probably had some kind of panic attack. I mean, it was the anniversary of the Longest Day. And on top of that, there was football.

Danny and I had always dreamed of playing for Cambridge Academy. If we won the game next week, there was a glimmer of hope: it would always be hard to get trials, but a tiny chance was better than no chance.

I was just stressed out. I must have been.

It was easy to forget about it in Art, because Mrs. Bridges constantly watched you and if you stopped working for more than a few seconds, she would come over and ask questions like, "What's so interesting that it's stopping you from drawing that apple?"

In PE we played rounders, and the only thing on my mind was trying to smack it farther than Slogger, which was practically impossible.

Then English came around.

I made sure I got a window seat because Mrs. Cole always likes to go on and on for the first twenty minutes. This room had a good view of the football pitches, at least.

I was just sitting down when she flung open the door and strode in, singing, "Shakespeare!"

A couple of kids groaned. I knew how they felt. Shakespeare? It was impossible to understand, even with all the notes down the side that explained what was going on.

Mrs. Cole scribbled Shakespeare on the board in big letters, then underlined it with a flourish. "What's not to love about that?" she said, bouncing all the way to her desk. She picked up a book and tapped its front cover, beaming round at the class.

Danny caught my eye. He made a gun with his fingers and pretended to blow his brains out. Trying to stifle a laugh, I shoved my hands over my mouth and turned away—

Then froze. My gut . . . it was twisting and turning, just like last night. It swelled up like a balloon, floating higher and higher.

My breath caught in my throat.

One minute I was staring into the courtyard, and the next there *was* no courtyard. No classroom at all. No carpet under my feet. Just dry, barren ground. A fierce wind stirred up clouds of dust that hung in the stinking air, making me gag and retch. A sudden Caw! rang out. With a flutter of black feathers, a crow shot into the gloomy sky.

I opened my mouth to speak, but no words came out. My throat tightened, my stomach clenched in shock. I tried to breathe, but my lungs weren't working. It was like I was strapped in to a ride I couldn't see, spinning round and round and round.

Then, as quickly as the dead world appeared, it vanished.

My mind whirled, filling with colors. I pressed the palms of my hands into my eyes, trying to shut out the blinding light.

"M-miss," I stammered, clutching my stomach. *Please don't be sick*, I thought. *Not here.*

Now that the rush of colors in my head was clearing, the classroom came back into focus.

I turned to the board. Shakespeare was scribbled across it, underlined three times. Was I dreaming? I must have been. I couldn't think of another explanation.

Automatically, I reached for my face, my hair, and—

No! It was wrong again.

I glanced at the window, but it was too bright to find my reflection. Dreading what I'd find, I opened my pencil tin and stared into the gleaming underside of the lid.

"No," I muttered, my mouth hanging open. I shot out of my seat and clattered into Dean's table. But even though every pair of eyes was locked on me, they weren't shocked like I thought they would be. They were just giggling because I'd interrupted the lesson.

"What's going on?" Mrs. Cole said.

"I . . . I'm sorry, Miss," I said, pinching my hair, the blond hair that wasn't mine and yet was on my head for the second time in two days.

"Is there a problem?" she trilled. "Have you got lice?"

Some of the class burst out laughing. I ignored them.

"No, Miss," I said, sitting slowly back down.

Couldn't they see?

*I'm going mad*, I thought. *This can't be happening.* I turned to Danny, but he only shrugged and made the kind of face that said: *STOP BEING SO WEIRD.*

"Well, if you don't mind, Owen, can we get back to Shakespeare?"

The singsongy voice was gone now.

"Yeah . . . sorry, Miss."

I couldn't concentrate for the rest of the lesson. I kept glancing at my reflection to see if my features had changed back, but they never did. I thought back to the photo last night and wished I hadn't deleted it. My face was different in it, I knew it was, and it was happening again now. But if that was true, then why could no one else see it?

When the lesson finally ended, I grabbed Danny in the corridor. "Do I look different?" I blurted, eyes wide to let him know that I wasn't messing around.

"What? No . . . but you're acting a bit strange, mate. Are you all right?"

I turned, unable to look at him as the lie formed on my tongue.

"Yeah. Yeah, I'm fine."

By the end of lunch, my features had changed back, but that didn't stop me worrying. I walked down to PE with

Danny, trying really hard to listen as he went through set plays and tactics for next week's game. But it was so hard to focus on what he was saying.

I wanted to beat Westfield as much as he did, but after what happened in English, more than anything I just wanted to figure out what was going on.

"There's a video of them on YouTube," Danny said. "I think one of the players' dads must have uploaded it. They try to play the offside trap, but if we can lure them in, I reckon I can have that number three . . ."

"Nice," I said.

That dream—if that was what it was—happened so suddenly. What if another one struck in training? The whole team would think I was nuts.

"Earth to Smithy," Danny said, wafting his hands in front of my face.

"Sorry," I mumbled, snapping out of my thoughts.

The clattering of studs filled the sports hall as we approached the main entrance to the changing room. We got into our gear and ran out onto the field.

"Three lines!" Mr. Matthews bellowed.

We warmed up, then broke down into drills, running round cones and hopping ropes. Normally I was quick on my feet—this sort of stuff should have been easy. But when I tried to stop and spin round a cone to get a good burst, I lost my balance. And I got tangled up and tripped in the rope ladder we were supposed to speed through.

"Focus, Smithy," Mr. Matthews said, but the more I tried to focus, the harder it got.

It all came back—the stench, the crow, the dusty air. It filled my mind and I bent over, stomach churning. I clenched my teeth, desperately fighting off the sick feeling.

When it came to the practice game, I didn't score a single goal. I barely even hit the net.

Mr. Matthews pulled me aside as the rest of the team headed back to get changed.

"Is something up, Smithy?" he said.

"No, Sir, it's just—"

"I need you at your sharpest on Wednesday. The team needs you."

"I know, sir. It won't . . . it won't happen again," I said, turning away because how could I stop it? I didn't even feel that weird dream coming earlier. And that meant it could happen again without my stopping it.

"I've been talking to the academy," he said. "They're coming, Owen. If we get to the quarter finals, they'll take a look. They'll send a scout."

I looked up then. His eyes were wide, and I could see myself reflected in them. I imagined walking through the entrance to a giant football stadium, me and Danny, the floodlights shining down on us. The flash of cameras in the crowd.

Then the stadium crumbled to dust, and all around me the ground was barren and dead.

I staggered back, breathing fast. I had to tell Dad what was happening to me. If this was all in my head, then I needed counseling more than he did.

# 6

When I got home, Dad was outside in the garden, talking to Clive over the fence. Our next-door neighbor was the kind of guy who could go on for hours, even if you were trying to end the conversation.

But for once it was Dad doing all the talking. And even though the not-me in the mirror kept flashing in my mind, a wave of happiness washed over me. The writing must have been working already, because I hadn't seen him this talkative in months.

Just then Dad looked back at the kitchen window. He smiled when he saw me, and raised a hand. I waved back, excitement fluttering in my stomach. I couldn't believe how good it was to see him smile like that.

"I've been meaning to say thanks," Dad said, coming in through the back door and closing it with a loud *clunk*.

"What for?"

"Getting me off my backside. Forcing me to go to see someone. I actually went today, you'll be pleased to know."

"I didn't force you," I said, but realizing he'd actually gone made my stomach ripple in excitement. Dad hadn't been himself for so long, but he'd only been to counseling once and already he was changing. I crossed my fingers and toes, praying that it could *keep* working.

"Artistic Healing," Dad said. "I would never have believed it. I'm still not sure I do. But I showed the counselor what I'm working on, and she convinced me to keep going. She said writing can be a powerful window to the soul that helps heal all wounds." He made a face, and I laughed.

"That's great," I said, and I really meant it.

Dad washed his hands in the sink, and the water turned brown with mud. "How was school?"

"Okay."

"Not giving me any more than that, eh?"

"I didn't really do much. I just . . ." I studied his face, the wrinkles around his eyes, the whiskery stubble on his cheeks. For one brief moment, seeing Dad smile had knocked all the worries out of my head. But now that I was away from the pitch, the memory of the daydream came creeping back. I had to tell Dad about the way I kept changing. Maybe he'd understand. He'd know if they really were dreams or . . . something worse. He'd know what to do. But as I looked at him, at the eagerness in his eyes and the expectant smile on his lips, the words ghosted away.

How did you talk about something so crazy? I didn't know where to begin.

I clenched my teeth, hating myself for being so scared.

"I just felt a bit ill," I said.

"Oh," he said. "Are you feeling okay now? Do you want me to take your temperature?"

"I'm fine. How's Clive?" I asked, changing the subject.

Dad dried his hands on the tea towel, but when he turned back he looked lost. "He wants to take me to a beer festival. I don't know, though. They're so loud. So many people."

"I could go with you," I said. "At school it's really loud sometimes. But I just talk to Danny, and after a while the rest of the noise gets drowned out. Maybe you could talk to me."

"Maybe," he said. He went to the fridge and grabbed a bottle of beer. There was a hiss and a crack, and wisps of gas drifted away from the open lid.

"What do you fancy for dinner tonight? Fish and chips?"

He must have seen the look on my face, because he set the bottle down, locking his eyes on mine. "I know we haven't had a proper meal in a while. And it's my fault. I just . . ." He sighed. "How about we cook something now, eh? You and me, together in the kitchen. Cooking maestros!"

"Yeah," I said, trying not to laugh at the look on his face. "Yeah, okay."

He ruffled my hair and gave me a playful squeeze.

"We haven't got much in, but I've got all the stuff for Juicy Lucy burgers," Dad went on, raiding the cupboards and dumping ingredients on the table. Then he looked back, his smile faltering. "Er—are you okay, Owen?"

"I'm fine," I said. I hadn't thought about food all the way home, but now that we had the chance to eat a proper dinner my stomach grumbled.

We made our special burgers, where the cheese oozed out of the middle, and grilled the veg to go with them. Then we sat down and turned on the TV—some documentary about airplanes—and even though we were both quiet, it wasn't a bad quiet, like when no one can think of anything to say and all you want to do is leave the room. It was a good quiet.

On the show they were following a plane that had crashed in the sea, and using modern technology to recreate what happened to it before, during, and after the accident. The presenter held up something that looked like a large metal cylinder. They called it a *black box* even though it was bright red. Apparently it had two different location devices on it—one radio beacon to be used on dry land and one pinger that activated automatically when it made contact with water.

"I love stuff like this," Dad said. "Fascinating, isn't it?" I didn't really find it that fascinating at all. It was just nice to be sitting with Dad, spending some time together. "Hey, why don't we go to an air show sometime? We haven't been since you were really little. Do you remember that one in Hastings?"

"Yeah," I said. How could I forget? I must have only been five or six, but they had ten Spitfires flying overhead, one of the largest displays there'd been since the war. I still remember the sound they made rumbling past us. The commentator said they flew like angels who'd left their wallets in the clouds. I didn't really know what it meant then—I still didn't—but at the same time, it kind of made sense. "Yeah, I'd like that."

I turned away to cover up the grin that was splitting my face. All this time, I'd hoped and hoped that Dad going to counseling would help, but it was one thing hoping it and another thing seeing it. I couldn't bring up the weird dream now. Not when he was in such a good mood.

Before I went to bed that night, I checked the bathroom mirror again. I held my breath as I looked into the glass, but it was just me blinking back in the reflection.

*Just a dream,* I told myself. It had to be. A stupid day-dream. Or day-nightmare, more like. Maybe it was a good thing I couldn't bring myself to tell Dad.

It probably wouldn't happen again, would it?

I couldn't have been more wrong.

# 7

The next morning, I looked for Dad in the kitchen. There was a teaspoon on the counter and the smell of toast still lingered, but the room was empty. The hall was quiet too.

Then I noticed the light was on in his study, so I went over to check on him.

"Couldn't sleep," he explained, when I knocked on the door. "Thought I'd get a head start on the writing, see how it goes."

"Nice one," I said.

I'd always *hoped* that the counseling would get him working like he used to—you know, to keep his mind busy—but I never imagined he'd be this keen. He didn't even write this early in the morning with his first book.

I ate breakfast on my own, watching kids' cartoons. As I got ready for school, I kept thinking about football. I was so useless yesterday. I didn't know what had got into me. I'd have to make sure I scored loads of goals today.

I opened the front door and was just walking down the drive when I heard a shout.

"WATCH OUT!"

I glanced up—

The next few seconds happened so fast they almost seemed slow. My throat tightened. I tried to move, but my legs were glued to the spot. My eyes widened as I saw the bike speeding toward me, brakes squealing. The front wheel locked and the back rose up, up, up, arcing through the air and flinging the rider right out of the seat.

Part of me wanted to try to catch the man so he wouldn't crash into the road. The other part of me needed to get out of the way. The two parts combined and I froze. At the last possible second I jerked out of the way, but the handlebars jabbed me hard in the ribs and I fell back, clattering into the recycling bins.

Garbage bags scattered over the road, spilling food containers and milk cartons all around me.

A sharp pain shot through my palms where the asphalt had ripped off the skin.

My gut twisted as I pushed myself onto my hands and knees, willing myself not to throw up.

"Are you okay?" said a voice across the street. "Young man?"

I didn't look up, didn't dare reply in case opening my mouth made it worse.

Then, just as suddenly as it began, the twisting and churning stopped. I blinked, rubbing my eyes on my sleeve to stop them watering.

At first I didn't realize anything had changed . . .

Then I started to notice things. The bike was gone. The man riding it was nowhere to be seen. And whoever was calling across the street must have run off quickly, because there was no one about. The streets were empty. And the streets round here were *never* empty. But it wasn't just that . . . there were no buses or cars, either.

The houses were in the same place, but they were broken, blackened, covered in dust and muck. The windows were smashed and boarded up. The bricks looked as if they'd been burned. If I hadn't been looking at them a few seconds ago, I wouldn't have guessed they were houses at all.

An acrid smell filled my nostrils. I staggered to my feet, turning round and round in shock.

*What's going on?*

"We've got to move," said a voice beside me.

I jumped and spun round, breathing quickly.

A boy was staring at me urgently. He looked about my age, maybe eleven or twelve. His clothes were grubby and mud stained and he clutched something tightly to his chest. No, not some*thing*. Lots of somethings. Cans of food and an old CD and a book.

Dillon. That was his name. It drifted from the back of my mind and hung there, burning bright. But how could I know that when I'd never seen him before?

I must have been daydreaming again. But how could I have been, when I'd been so close to getting knocked over by that bike? You didn't just fall asleep or drift off like that, did you? My heart was only just calming down.

An explosion of noise made me look up.

Cawing and screeching, cackling, crying out.

Something black rose on the horizon. Maybe they were crows, like the one that landed next to me when I had daydreamed in school.

They started off like a stain, pooling out, rising up into the gray. Then they spread out, until they weren't just a black mark in the distance. They became a cloud, a huge cloud, getting bigger and bigger by the second.

*They're not birds*, I thought. *They can't be birds. No birds fly like that.*

The wails grew louder. The black stain was so big now that it blotted out the sun. And it was getting closer. It was coming this way.

"*Move,*" Dillon growled.

"W-what is it?" I stammered. As it closed in, it spread out, oozing over the sky like spilled ink. Whatever it was, I couldn't take my eyes off it.

"The Darkness," Dillon said, his eyes narrowing. He looked me up and down, a confused expression on his face. Then he shook himself and moved away, glancing from building to building. "Where's Iris? We've got to run!"

Iris? As soon as he said the name, an image of her flashed in my mind. I'd seen her before. I . . . I knew her. But how could I? I'd never met anyone called Iris in my life.

"I need to get back for Dad," I said. "I need to see if he's okay." Something must have happened when I got knocked over. Something bad. And he was still in his study. He wouldn't know anything about it. I had to get back and warn him.

Suddenly a whirlwind of thoughts exploded in my head. Images and places and people and things. Things I'd never seen before, things I'd never known.

But standing there . . . Standing there, it felt like I'd known them all my life.

It was like I'd become a different person. Like I wasn't Owen Smith at all . . .

I glanced down—

And cried out in shock. My school blazer, my trousers and shirt and tie—they'd vanished again. Instead, I was wearing the same kind of rags that Dillon had on.

I held out my hands and examined them under the fading light. They were too big. The fingers were thicker than normal. They weren't my hands. They couldn't be my hands.

Panicking, I felt my hair. It was long again.

*What's happening to me?*

Another screech echoed off the ruined houses, and I whirled round, each breath getting faster and faster. But there was only the wasteland. Only the Darkness.

Dillon grabbed my wrist and dragged me into the barren road.

"We've got to get into the light," he said. "Run!"

The high wailing was so loud now I could feel it as well as hear it.

Dillon ran. I hesitated, turning back to my house—

But it wasn't there. All that was left was a pile of brick in the vague shape of a building. The garden was lined with the hollow husks of long-dead trees. The grass was blackened and dead.

Adrenaline surged through me and I pelted after Dillon.

The scream ripped through the air just as I caught up with him. *The Darkness*, I thought. Is that where it was coming from? But then I heard the scream again, and I realized it sounded different to the high wailing. It sounded like—

Like a girl.

She was there, fifty yards behind us. Iris.

"Help!" she called, stumbling toward us.

She was carrying too much in her arms. She wasn't moving fast enough.

I skidded to a stop, kicking up swirling clouds of dust. The Darkness covered the whole horizon like a raging storm, tendrils lashing out at the dead trees, licking at the rubble and rocks.

It was closing in—fast.

There was no way Iris was going to make it. And if I went back for her, it'd probably get me too. Dillon's desperate voice echoed in my mind. *Run.* I glanced back again, but he was long gone, rushing toward a dome of light in the distance.

What would happen if the Darkness touched us? I plunged into the rush of memories, but the fog in my head made it too hard to see them.

"Help me!" Iris yelled again.

What was she holding? Why couldn't she just let it go? Surely nothing could be as important as getting away from that cloud. I took a deep breath and ran back toward her.

"Just drop it!" I shouted over the whipping wind. "Let it go! We've got to run!"

"I can't!" Her foot caught and she stumbled. I reached out to steady her, and my hands brushed against the two plastic containers she held, filled with sloshing liquid. "We've got to get these back to camp. If we don't—"

But whatever she was about to say got cut off. An ear-splitting cry filled the air, like a bird of prey but a hundred times worse.

Iris's eyes grew wide with fear.

I didn't dare look up at the storm. I didn't want to know how close it was. Gritting my teeth, I grabbed the containers off Iris and held one under each arm.

Then I ran.

I ran as fast as I could toward the light. That must have been the camp she mentioned. It was hard to make out from so far away, but I could see people moving inside the dome.

Iris darted alongside me, her hair whipping around her face.

I could see Dillon in the distance. He was miles away now. He'd almost reached the camp. He was going to make it. But we—

I glanced back quickly, just to check.

It was right on us, bubbling and boiling, reaching out with flickering fingers. Something snapped. There was a snarl, like a rabid dog. An orange gleam appeared and vanished again back into the clouds.

Desperately I willed my legs to move faster. Every breath felt icy cold, stabbing my throat. But the Darkness was closing in too quick.

"What happens if we touch it?" I panted, glancing at Iris.

And right away I knew it was the wrong thing to say. Her forehead creased. There was a look in her eyes like she was trying to figure out if I was joking or not.

"Jack—," she said breathlessly.

But another screech cut her off, so loud it made me stumble. I caught myself, breathing heavily, trying to get away from the storm even though I knew I couldn't, even though it was impossible.

Jack. That was my name.

*But I'm not!* I thought. I was Owen Smith. Just plain old Owen Smith, and I didn't belong here. I should have been back at home, back in the real Cambridge, where there was grass in the fields and leaves on the trees and buildings that were full of life.

The screech rang out again as the storm closed in and I shut my eyes tight, trying to picture home, wishing I could just wake up from this nightmare, kick a ball around in the garden with Dad, *anything*, as long as it wasn't this. A cold feeling seeped out from my heart, down my arms and legs, tingling my fingers and toes.

My mind filled with images again, but not strange memories that I'd never seen before, like Dillon's name and the Darkness.

They were—

They were mine. Owen's.

"Mum," I said, trying to imagine the sight of her healthy face, her real face, because I knew now what memories were coming and there was nothing I could do to stop them.

*I was standing outside the hospital ward. Inside, Dad held Mum in his arms. They didn't know I was there. They thought I'd gone to buy them drinks.*

*Even though Mum had been in pain for months, she never cried.*

*But when I left the room, she must have given in.*

*She must have broken down.*

*Because she wasn't fighting now. The tears flowed down her face.*

The memory shattered. I was surrounded by Darkness again, breathing faster and faster. My throat was dry and tight. My eyes burned. That memory—it felt so real. Like I was living it again. Like I was there.

A long, thin tendril of Darkness reached out, lurching toward me. All I could hear was whispering. Soft, quiet whispering, repeating the same words again and again. *I'm so sorry, Owen.* It was Mum's voice. The fog in my head grew stronger than ever. I couldn't shake the weight in my chest. I stepped back, but my knees buckled and collapsed . . .

*The machines around Mum beeped and beeped. The nurses rushed me out—*

*I looked at her through the window, saw her white face, her sunken eyes—*

*Now we were back at home and she was in bed, gagging and retching—*

A sudden roar jolted me back and I dropped the containers to cover my ears in shock. High, never-ending screaming, like a hundred cats fighting in the night. But it wasn't the Darkness, like I expected it to be. It was a truck, headlights blaring. Swirls of dust twisted and twined, hanging in the golden beams. The light stabbed into the seething storm cloud, and where it touched, the Darkness sizzled and popped. The clouds pulled back, recoiling at the edge of the light.

It couldn't get any closer. It couldn't penetrate the headlights.

I gulped desperately, breathing hard. But the relief didn't last long. Because lying in the dirt, a few yards in front of the truck, was Iris.

She wasn't moving. Fresh panic bubbled up inside me, but it was distant and close at the same time, as if it wasn't just coming from me.

The truck door opened and a man jumped out. He held a flashlight in his hand, and shone it at the Darkness, making it scream louder. Then he cast the light over Iris.

When she was running, her hair trailed like fire behind her, but now . . . now it was limp and lifeless. The man knelt beside her and brushed a loose strand out of her face. He slid his arms under her back, lifted her up, and took her to the truck. He laid her along the backseat, then turned to me.

"Did it get you?" he said, scanning my face. He had short black hair and wild, silvery stubble. His eyes were dark and lined, like Dad's got after the Longest Day. "Did you touch it?"

"What?" I said, trying to get hold of the thoughts in my head. Did he mean the Darkness? If I did, would I even remember? The way it gleamed and cackled, those memories—a shiver ran through me even thinking about them. "I don't think so," I said, watching him carefully. "It was about to get us, but then . . ."

"It's okay," he said. "You're safe now. Come on, let's get back to camp."

# 8

The engine roared into life. The man floored the accelerator, yanking the wheel and spinning us round to face the camp. Lights had sprung up all around it, shining into the sky. If it'd had walls, it would have looked like a football stadium.

There was a crackle on the dashboard and I looked down. It was some kind of radio, like in police cars. A voice shouted through the bursts of static.

"Quinn, you there?"

"Yeah," the man said. "I'm here."

"It's started earlier than before. It's coming faster too."

"I know," Quinn muttered, dodging the blackened husk of a fallen tree. "Just get the perimeter up." His eyes flicked to the rearview mirror. He licked his lips, and gripped the steering wheel harder as the truck sped forward.

I twisted in my seat to get a better view. Iris was slumped in the back, unconscious. Behind us red dust clouds billowed up, only to be swallowed by the storm. The Darkness lashed out, chittering madly, but every time it got close to the rear lights it sizzled and pulled back.

I could hear sirens now, just like the ones in war films, the ones that wailed high and low and high and low. Outside the window, the Darkness overtook us, fingers of rippling black slamming against the glass. Fear stabbed through the fog in my head. I gripped the seat so hard my knuckles turned white, and willed the truck to go faster.

Quinn flicked on to full beam, and in front of us the Darkness peeled away.

I looked down at my rags again. The elbows were torn, the knees mud stained. But a few minutes ago, I was in my school uniform leaving the house. This wasn't my world . . . it was like I was trapped inside a horror movie. I didn't understand it—any of it—and the more I thought about it, the more light-headed I felt.

"How can this be happening?" I whispered, more to myself than anything.

Quinn glanced at me sideways.

"You're sure it didn't touch you?" he said.

How could I tell? It was just a storm cloud, wasn't it? And yet—

It was so much more.

"I don't think so," I said finally.

We were approaching the center of a city now. Light flooded out from cracks in the abandoned buildings and holes in the broken roofs. Every street lamp was on too. All along the road people were manning huge floodlights, hooked up to even bigger generators, which glowed green and thrummed with life. They all shone up, into the sky, creating a huge dome of piercing white light. And we were heading straight for it.

A blood-chilling shriek split the gloom as the Darkness lashed out one last time. But the truck was too fast. We pulled away, getting closer and closer to the light—

And then we burst through the protective dome, skidding along the narrow streets.

As we shot through the gap between two broken-down buildings, I realized . . . this place, whatever it was, was just like the Cambridge city center. Well, not *just* like it, because Cambridge was alive and green and filled with people, and its buildings were so pristine that you could buy them on postcards. I didn't think these buildings would ever be on postcards. None of them were whole. Almost all of them had been reduced to piles of broken brick and rubble. Every now and then we passed a wall that still resembled a shopfront, but the windows were smashed and the roof above them was caved in. Out of all of the holes shone dazzling light, adding more strength to the barrier.

The storm slammed into the light, but it couldn't follow us, it couldn't break through. There was a hiss and a crackle as the jet-black clouds rippled over us. Inside the dome, it was as clear as day, but above us the Darkness turned the sky into never-ending night.

I'd been gripping the seat so hard my knuckles ached, but now I let go and flexed them, working out the pain. My hands were shaking, so I sat on them to cover it up. My rags were drenched in sweat.

I didn't dare let my guard down. We may have escaped the storm, but we were hardly safe.

Quinn slowed the truck down near an open space, which, I realized now, would have been the market square in the real Cambridge. I stared wide-eyed at the buildings around us, all of them pumping out great beams of light, the exact opposite of those stories you heard about the war. In wartime, families had to turn off their lights so they couldn't be spotted by enemy planes flying overhead. These houses *wanted* to be seen now. They wanted to be big and bright.

Around the market, some shops had been patched up and repaired. Cloth canopies stretched out from crumbling walls, with stalls spread out underneath them. In the middle of the square was a large table with a steaming pot on top. All around it, other tables were loaded with books and CDs, and the kind of stuff you'd get at a charity shop.

"You found some gas," Quinn said, and before I could tell him that it wasn't me, it was Iris, he went on, "That's good. That's really good. I'll take it to the refilling station. You two need to get to Cleansing."

I nodded, even though I had no idea what he was talking about. Cleansing? I didn't want to go anywhere but home. This place . . . The blackened buildings, the lifeless earth. It made my skin itch. I pinched myself, trying to wake up.

Nothing.

Just a sharp pain and a red mark on my skin.

I didn't know you could feel pain in dreams . . .

The truck pulled up and Quinn leapt out. Iris stirred as he carried her out and helped her to stand. She was alive, at least. She hadn't—

She hadn't died. That was what I was going to say. But the thought felt strange. Could a storm really do that? Could it kill? Where had I got that idea from? Then I thought back to the way it screeched, the way it moved, and suddenly it didn't feel so stupid.

"W-what . . ." Iris stammered.

"Don't worry," Quinn said. "You're safe. You both are."

I hesitated, then slid out of the truck into the buzz and hum of the electric light and the droning wail of the siren. It was still blaring now, even though the Darkness was trapped outside the barrier. I watched as the storm clouds billowed, blacker than midnight, hanging over the camp like the shadow of some giant spaceship.

Those memories . . .

Mum in the hospital, crying in Dad's arms.

Somehow the storm had dragged them back up.

I needed to get away, to try to find a way to wake myself up. Pinching myself obviously wasn't going to do it, but maybe something else would.

A wave of nausea flooded through me just as another man came rushing up to us from the square, muttering in a low voice to Quinn. I squinted at him, eyes streaming. I thought I recognized his voice from the radio in Quinn's truck.

"Get these two to Cleansing," Quinn said. "Then check the lights. Make sure we're secure. I'll be with you in a minute."

My legs buckled. I clutched my stomach, trying to steady it. I staggered. The last thing I saw was the concern in Quinn's eyes as the ground reared up and smacked me in the face.

# 9

I opened my eyes.

High-pitched ringing filled my ears.

I blinked, and looked blearily around.

I half expected to be back in bed, or in the hospital. But this wasn't my room, I knew that much. The walls were bare and crumbling. As my vision cleared, the room came into focus. The ceiling was half crumbled, the holes patched up with canvas and wood. Shafts of light pierced through the gaps, picking out motes of dust all around me.

But that wasn't the strangest thing. The strangest thing was the TV, set against the wall, directly in front of me. Why would you have a TV in such an abandoned-looking room?

*Where am I?*

My heart quickening, I opened my mouth to call out, but my throat was so dry the words got caught. That ringing! It wasn't just in my ears, it was in my mind too. Constant wailing, a rush of jumbled thoughts.

I tried to move—

And that was when the panic kicked in.

There was something clamped to my wrists.

My legs wouldn't budge either. I strained and pulled, but I was locked in place.

Deep breaths. Calm down. *It's all right*, I thought, even though it didn't feel all right. How could it possibly be when I was locked in a chair in some kind of—

Some kind of what?

Prison?

"Hello?" I said, forcing the words out, but my voice was so quiet. "Hello?"

Nothing. Only the heavy silence and the dust.

The quiet made my pulse hammer harder and harder. Where was everyone? First I got chased by that storm, and now this. I thought back to what Quinn had said. *Get him to Cleansing.* Is that what this was? Nothing in here looked very clean. And my rags . . . they hadn't done anything about them. I looked as if I'd never even heard of a bath.

"Let me out!" I yelled.

"Ah, you're awake," said a woman's voice. "There's no need to worry, Jack, this is completely normal procedure."

*Jack?* I thought, my mind reeling. Everything was still wrapped in that thick, pressing fog. Something about it sounded wrong. "That's not my name," I said. I tried again to move, to wriggle out, but the ropes wouldn't budge.

"Of course it is. You've been touched by the Darkness. The lemon balm oil should see to the burns, but if your memory has been affected, we'll have to act quickly . . ."

"Lemon balm? Why have you got that here?" It seemed an odd thing to have in a camp where everything was so dead. How had they even got it?

"Don't worry, Jack, it's perfectly normal to feel panicked after exposure. We've been through this dozens of times before. The Darkness has a habit of jarring memories out of your head, when it drags up the horrible ones you try to forget. Lemon balm is a miracle medicine. The pre-Darks used it for alleviating Alzheimer's, as well as treating cuts and burns. Thankfully it works just as well now, or else we'd be in rather big trouble."

The woman moved into my line of sight. Her clothes were dark and dirt smeared, and she had a mask over her nose and mouth. Her blonde hair was tied back in a bun, and her cold gray eyes made the hairs on the back of my neck squirm. Instinctively I tried to move again, to back up, to run. But she didn't come any closer. She moved to the far wall and switched on the TV screen.

"What do you remember?" the woman said, turning back to me.

I stopped struggling against the chair and focused on trying to think. What *did* I remember? Everything happened so fast after I got hit by that bike, and it didn't help that every time I tried to make sense of anything the fog in my head thickened.

But something told me she wasn't talking about my life. Owen's life. She called me Jack, just like Quinn had. I wasn't Owen here, not to these people.

"I . . . I don't know," I said.

"Let's start with the City," she pressed, not taking her eyes off me.

"Which city? What do you mean?"

"*The* City." She frowned. "Our City. Our home."

Growing desperate, I tried to find those thoughts again, the ones that weren't mine. They had to come from somewhere. If I could just access them again, maybe I'd be able to figure out what was going on. The woman's face was set in an expression that might have been concern, but it disappeared quickly, as if it was too hard to overcome the sternness of her eyes and mouth. She turned to the TV and pressed a button on the screen.

With a flicker of static, a series of images flashed up. First a building—no, a whole load of buildings—dozens of faces, a raging storm cloud. Each one shot by so fast it was almost impossible to see. Recognition flickered in the back of my mind, the same place where the thoughts that weren't mine had bubbled up earlier.

Was this the City she was talking about?

"Keep your eyes on the screen," the woman said, moving away. I turned to check what she was doing. There was a monitor on the side of the room, a bit like the one they'd had beside Mum in the hospital. "The *screen*," the woman repeated. "I can't help you if you don't want to be helped."

A soft hissing sounded somewhere above me.

And that smell . . . lemons and mint. Was it some kind of lemon balm gas?

"What are you doing to me?" I wrenched my arms against the chair again, but all it did was send red-hot pain stabbing into my wrists. "Let me out!"

"You'll be let out once we know you're safe," the woman said.

I had to get out. I *needed* to get out. But there was nothing I could do. They had me trapped. Trying frantically to control the panic ripping through me, I forced myself to look at the screen.

A movie was playing, showing archive footage from—

No, that couldn't be right. The year said 2024.

Was this the future? Had I somehow time-traveled when I got hit by the bike? That was impossible . . . but then, I thought, as the footage played, everything about this place was impossible.

A montage of shaky phone videos showed the first storm hitting. Newscasters detailed the spread of huge dust clouds as they swept across the world and cut off access to nuclear reactors in every country, destabilizing them, allowing dangerous levels of radiation to leak out. I watched wide-eyed as the clouds shifted, mutated, and grew.

The storm changed from dust to Darkness and chewed through buildings and forests alike, reshaping the landscape like a child with a lump of clay.

It was just like a disaster movie. Except this one was real, wasn't it? No, not real. My life was real. Dad and school and the National School Football Championships. Those things were real.

But I had seen the Darkness right up close. I felt what it did to me. And this room, this chair, my stinging wrists— right now, they were definitely real.

The machine on the wall beeped.

Out of the corner of my eye I saw the woman making notes.

The footage cut to London. It showed people in battered ruins, building shelters in the shadow of Wembley Stadium. They carved out homes for themselves, fighting off the storm with weapons made from the stadium floodlights. My eyes were straining to keep up with the flashing images, but I couldn't look away. I saw London grow until it couldn't grow any more, the conditions deteriorating as space ran out, people sleeping in cramped, dirty rooms. Day and light lost all meaning. There was only the permanent dark, punctuated by the electric glow of the safe haven in London. Occasional pockets of daylight disrupted the storm, but it was impossible to tell how long they'd last. The survivors adapted, dividing into classes, with each fulfilling a specific role. Was London the City the woman was talking about?

The newscaster appeared onscreen again.

"The Duplication Act, created by the Council of Marshals two years ago, allows three crews to be created," she said, as, behind her, people boarded three great airships.

"The Icarus projects 1, 2 and 3 are launching as a last resort, a desperate bid to find hope. Each is led by a Marshal and two adults from each class, who will be in charge of the duplicates. Their mission is simple, but incredibly dangerous: discover new safe locations for us to live. The children on board, all of them illegal seconds and thirds, have a choice: live in exile, or try to save the human race."

Duplication Act? Seconds and thirds? My mind raced, trying to piece it all together . . .

A memory flickered in the back of my mind, but I knew it wasn't mine. *There wasn't enough room for everyone. So women were permitted only one son and one daughter. The Duplication Act made second sons and second daughters illegal. The people of the City needed volunteers for their mission, so they made a law to force duplicates into the Icarus program.*

The images on the TV flashed. I watched the Icarus airships fly out of the City, carrying huge crates below them. Icarus 1 headed south, toward the coast, Icarus 2 swung north, and Icarus 3 ventured east.

And suddenly I knew. I didn't know how, but I did. It was there in my mind, as if I'd lived in this world my whole life, as if Owen was no more than a dream of a dream.

We were Icarus 3. We were duplicates. And we were here to save the City. To find a new safe haven from the Darkness. We were Stormwalkers.

My heart quickened at the thought. I understood the classes more clearly now. LRP were enforcers, whose job it was to secure the perimeter and try to track down any other survivors. Hunters foraged in the ruins to salvage anything that could be useful. Farmers specialized in growing food that could withstand the stress of daily storms. Scholars safeguarded the country's history and passed the knowledge on to future generations, and the Carers, well, they tried to keep everyone alive. The Stormwalkers didn't do anything *except* go out into the storm. They did the dirty work that you couldn't do in daylight, like gathering glowroot for research.

But here in camp, there weren't enough adults to fill all the usual roles, so we had to do a bit of everything. While LRP worked on trying to reestablish communication with the City and expanding the perimeter of the camp, we made the space we did have better by Farming and gathering important equipment, as well as keeping up with our usual Stormwalker duties.

In the City, we were illegal. But here, we had a chance to be heroes.

The video stopped, and the screen faded to black.

"You remember," said the woman. She approached me slowly, studying my face. "You do, don't you?"

I tried to speak, but the words got caught in my throat.

*Jack.* That was my name. The fog thinned and in its place memories flooded through me. Dad, at home in the City, and someone else too. A brother—Ayden. They hid me every time the guards came round to inspect our house—

*No.*

*That's not right*, I thought. *My name is Owen. Plain old Owen Smith.*

"Don't you?" the woman repeated firmly.

It felt like I was two people. Two sets of thoughts, two lives, all wrapped up in one body. I saw it all, like I was watching it on TV. Saw them take me when I was eight, and train me ready for this mission. Saw us flying through the storm and crash-landing in the ruins of Cambridge.

Suddenly the lemon and mint made me feel sick. It started in my stomach, twitching there, and rose up into my throat.

The woman was still looking at me, waiting for an answer.

I nodded.

"Okay," she said. She glanced at someone behind me, giving a silent command.

Rough hands untied the ropes binding me. "Get up," said a man's voice.

I hoisted myself out of the seat, arms shaking with the effort. My legs buckled as my weight shifted and I almost fell, but strong arms caught me.

I retched.

"Easy," the man said.

Leaning on him for support, I took a shaky step forward, then another. Before I could ask where we were going, a thought flashed, and I realized some part of me already knew.

I retched again, and this time I threw up. I crouched over the dirt and broken stone, my throat burning as it all came out. I wanted to curl up right there on the ground, but the man was already urging me on.

"The sooner we get this over with, the sooner you can be back out there," he said.

We picked our way over crumbled bricks and splintered wood on the dusty floor. I could hear the canvas above us rippling in the breeze. And another sound . . .

Something distant. Something cold. Something that turned my stomach.

There was a hiss as we left the Cleansing room, and suddenly powerful jets hit me from every direction. I spluttered and gasped as liquid streamed down my face, drenching the dirty rags that had replaced my school uniform.

When the jets shut down, the man took my arm again, gripping too hard. I wasn't going to fight against him. Not in this state.

Through another door, and now we emerged into a circular room, my sodden shoes squelching with every step. There was a lone chair in the middle of the floor. Opposite, a makeshift desk had two women sitting behind it. The man told me to sit down, and strode over to join the others.

"We're just going to ask you a few questions," he said. "Make sure your exposure to the Darkness hasn't had any lingering effects. If all goes well, you'll be back with the others in no time."

I shivered involuntarily, and it wasn't just because I was cold.

What would happen if it *didn't* go well?

"Full name?" said the woman on the right.

I traced the outline of my face again, just like I had in front of the mirror at home. This wasn't my body. Somehow, I was inside Jack. That must be why I could hear his thoughts, and see his memories as if they were my own.

But how could that be? Was this all in my head? When I saw the dead world in English, I must have fallen asleep somehow, because Mrs. Cole acted like I'd never left the room. But this time I got hit by a bike, didn't I? It was easy to fall asleep at school, but who falls asleep getting run over? Unless the bike knocked me unconscious. That could explain it . . .

I fought my way through to the thoughts that belonged to Jack. As I did so, everything linked to me—my real life in the living version of Cambridge—faded into the background. I let it go.

"Jack," I said automatically. "Er, Jack Spencer."

"I'm going to give you a number, Jack, and I'd like you to remember it as best you can. Are you ready? Three hundred and eighty-six. Have you got that?"

I nodded, wondering where this was going. I still felt so ill . . .

The second woman leaned forward, and the desk creaked under the weight of her elbows.

"Can you remember what you were doing before you got caught by the Darkness?"

I thought back to the moment the storm rippled up on the horizon. What *had* we been doing? That boy, Dillon, had loads of objects in his hands, and Iris was cradling the gasoline when she tried to escape. I needed to go back further—back before I found myself in this place, in this body.

My hand shot to my stomach, ready to fight the sick feeling as I flicked through the rush of thoughts, but as I did, the man picked up a pen and noted something down. I quickly snatched my hand away. Whatever this test was, I needed to pass it so I could get away. So I could find out how to get home.

"We were hunting for things," I said slowly. "I was looking for glass, Iris found some gasoline, and Dillon had some food."

"And do you remember," said the first woman, "what you saw, when the Darkness got too close? Did it speak to you? Did it show you anything in particular?"

"Er . . ."

I remembered. How could I forget?

Mum's face had been so real, as if she was right there, as if I could reach out and hug her.

But I couldn't say that, could I? I couldn't tell them the truth, because they'd realize something strange was going on. They'd put me through all this again, or worse.

If I just *twisted* it slightly . . .

"My family," I said, as an image of Jack's dad and brother floated before me again. "They were . . . they were dying."

"I'm sorry," said the man. "The Darkness can force us to relive our deepest fears, even ones we never knew we had. But your family is alive and safe. It's only a matter of time before the City picks up our signal. We'll be able to take evacuees soon enough."

There was silence for a while, as the three of them consulted notes. The woman from the video room came through and handed them something. They whispered among themselves, and I felt like some talent show contestant hoping the judges wouldn't all give me a no.

"What was your number?" the man said abruptly, looking up at me.

"My number? Oh—three hundred and eighty-six," I said, thankful that I didn't have to fight for that one. Looking for answers had made me light-headed and weak.

The man nodded, and checked off something on the page in front of him.

"Good. Very good. Well, everything seems to be in order. You're free to go, Jack. Take a few minutes' rest, then get changed. Try to be back to the timetable within the hour. Oh, and Jack? Don't let it get so close next time, eh? I know you Stormwalkers like to think you're invincible, but that was dangerously close, considering you didn't have your suit on."

"All right," I said, trying to keep all the questions from showing on my face.

They left the room together, and when I felt as if my legs could take my weight, I staggered after them, still dripping from whatever they had drenched me with in the hallway.

Outside, I breathed in the cold air of the electric night, my mind racing as fast as the storm flickering and flaring above me. If the storm first hit the world in 2024, then what year was it now? How long did it take for the City to launch the Icarus program?

*Decades*, came a thought from the back of my mind.

I shivered, knowing it couldn't have been mine. I took a deep breath, looking again at this world around me. I knew more about it and the Darkness, but I still wasn't any closer to figuring out *how* I got here.

And if I didn't know how I got here, how could I ever get back?

# 10

I hugged my arms close to my body, trying to keep warm.

*Go and get changed*, the man had said. Where on earth was I supposed to do that?

I could try to access Jack's memories again, but every time I did I felt like I was going to faint. My head was still reeling from everything I'd seen and heard. It seemed ridiculous to think that, not that long ago, I was getting ready for school.

I looked at my ruined surroundings. Rubble littered the empty floors. Paths had been cleared for people to move between them, but inside some of the buildings there was nothing but cobwebs and rocks. And the lights . . . they were everywhere. Even in the most destroyed spaces. Floodlights and spotlights, humming electronically as they beamed up into the sky, creating a huge protective barrier of light over the whole camp.

And above it, crackling and bubbling, was the storm.

*The Darkness.*

Gleaming light flickered inside it, making it look as though cruel faces leered down at the ruins. It was impossible to tell if it was day or night. Whenever the clouds slammed into the light barrier, they snarled and pulled back as if stung. Somehow, the storm couldn't get through.

I swallowed to ease the dryness of my throat. There was a stale taste in my mouth, as if I hadn't brushed my teeth for days. I wandered down a narrow alley, and suddenly I could see the Senate House. And King's College next to it. Well, the remains of them, anyway. These were the buildings I knew, the streets I grew up on. But they weren't my streets. My streets weren't dotted with craters and rubble.

I spun round, taking it all in.

And that was when I saw it.

It was as tall as me, although it wasn't human. It had tracks like a tank and a clear dome where its head should have been. It was some kind of . . . some kind of robot, moving debris out of the street with mechanical arms.

I closed my eyes, willing myself to wake up. Maybe if I tried as hard as I could, I'd open my eyes and be back on the side of the road, covered in rubbish. The cyclist would help me up and say, "Sorry!" and I could go to school and it would just be a normal day.

When I opened my eyes again, I was looking straight into someone else's.

"Whoa," I said, heart thumping. "Where did you come from?"

It was the girl from the storm. Iris. How could I have forgotten about her? Forgotten she almost died? But seeing her now, alive and well . . . my stomach floated in a way that felt alien—the kind of happiness that only struck when I was hanging out with Danny.

I was so startled that it took me a while to realize that she had been through Cleansing too. Wet mud streaked her cheeks and her threadbare clothes were sodden. Did I look as bedraggled as her?

"Thanks for helping me back there," she said.

"It's . . . er . . . it's okay," I said, even though I hadn't really done anything. I mean, I had woken up here so quickly, all I had time to do was panic.

"We should get back to the hall. If we're quick, we might be able to get to class in time."

She set off up the road. I hurried after her.

"Class?" That sounded too much like school to me. Even though I had no idea what was happening, I knew one thing: I was still in control of myself. This may have been a dream, but at least I could do what I wanted. And I did not want to go to class.

"Er, yes. Class? You know, the timetable we have to stick to every day of our lives," Iris said sarcastically, as if that explained everything.

The dirt on her face made the green of her eyes brighter than I remembered.

I didn't know what to say. Well, I *did* know what to say—I just didn't want to sound like an idiot. I just wanted to get out of here, to go back to being me. And I needed someone to help me.

"Iris, I'm not who you think I am."

Iris stopped and stared at me. "What are you talking about?"

"I'm not . . . look, I'm not Jack."

"Yeah, whatever, good one," she said, turning to walk off again.

"I mean it. I'm not him. I'm not from here at all."

"Jack, don't be ridiculous. I've trained with you since I was eight years old. I'm not in the mood for jokes."

"I know you're not. And I know you have. It's hard to explain . . ."

Iris glanced at the robot, then turned back to me and whispered furiously. "Stop messing around!"

"I'm not messing around! I'm not like you. I'm not from around here. I mean, Jack is . . . I can hear his thoughts, I can see what he's seen, but they're not my memories. They're his. And I need . . . I need to get out of here."

The robot trundled closer. Iris grabbed me and pulled me out of the road.

"Keep your voice down!" she hissed, narrowing her eyes at me. "If you keep going on like that, they'll send you to the Chamber."

"What do you mean? Who's *they*? And what's the Chamber?"

"You're not funny. I don't know what you're trying to do, but you can stop it now."

"I'm not trying to *do* anything," I said, struggling to keep quiet as frustration bubbled up inside me. "All I know is I woke up here in this place, and I want to get back. I just . . ."

I just what? How could Iris possibly help me? If this *was* a dream, I needed to wake myself up. An idea formed somewhere in the back of my mind. Maybe this wasn't a dream. Maybe it was a nightmare. And in nightmares, it was always a shock that woke you up.

I thought back to when the storm got close, the seething tendrils reaching out. The closer they got, the colder I grew. Those memories shot through me, clear and icy as the winter sea. If I got close to the Darkness again, maybe the fright would be enough.

"Sorry. Just forget I said anything," I said. I moved to walk away, but Iris grabbed my arm.

"Jack . . ." she said. "You're scaring me. If the Cleansing didn't work . . . please tell me you remember. I don't want them to take you away. I don't want you to become . . . to become Dreamless."

Just then the robot stopped. There was a camera in its domed head, and it whirred as it turned to face us.

"Hello . . . STORMWALKERS," it said, pausing clunkily between the words. "You should be in . . . CLASSROOM 3B for . . . HISTORY OF THE PRE-DARK WORLD."

"I know, we're going," Iris said, dragging me away from it. The camera rotated to follow us, then the robot went back to cleaning up rubble.

I pulled out of Iris's grip and backed away.

"Look, I don't know what you're talking about," I said, as kindly as possible. "I'm not supposed to be here. Normally when you have a nightmare, you wake up when you realize it's not real. But that's not working, so I need to find a way to get back."

"Jack . . ." she started to say, but I was already walking quickly away, looking for a route to the market square. "Don't think I won't report you, just because . . . just because we're friends. Jack, *please*! Don't make me call the guards! JACK!"

I ducked out of sight behind the nearest building, waiting to see if she would follow me, listening to the *thump-thump-thump* of my heart and the crackle of the Darkness above.

When I peeked round the corner, she'd gone.

And that robot thing—whatever it was—was still driving along the road.

The distant wailing siren had stopped. It must have been some kind of alarm to alert the camp to the danger. They were all here, living their lives, dealing with this every day. Just trying to stay alive so they could rescue the City and build a new home for their families.

Me . . . I'd prefer a lifetime of Shakespeare lessons over the Darkness.

I waited until I was sure Iris had gone, then crept through the ruined streets. The lights hummed around me, so bright I could see all the way to the edge of camp. In the middle of the dome was the market square. It was easy to recognize, because it was the only part of this dead world that still looked used.

The square was busier than the streets around it. Kids scurried to and fro, carrying containers and scrap metal or bartering at market stalls for food. Were all of them illegal duplicates like Jack was? Everyone wore the same dirty clothes, like a filthy school uniform. Above them, strung across the storm-eaten rooftops like washing lines, a series of wires emitted puffs of mist. I could smell the lemon balm from here.

And in the distance, behind the church's clock tower, stood the hollowed and crumbled building that made Cambridge what it was. King's College Chapel. In my world, it was tall and intricate and if you squinted you could make out little statues sitting in nooks and fine carving on the spires. Here, there were no spires. They'd crumbled and smashed on the road. The roof had caved in, and out if it now poured great beams of light.

Dad once told me you could climb that roof and see all the way to Ely. Here, you'd only see a hundred yards beyond the ruin, where the edge of the light met the endless black.

*Dad . . .*

A cold knot tightened in my stomach. If this was a dream, then it was getting worse. The one at school had only lasted a few seconds at most. I'd have to tell Dad now. He'd take me to see a doctor. They'd ask me all about Mum and the Longest Day and the L-word and I didn't want to talk about that, didn't want to even think about it, so I latched onto a happy memory and held it in my mind.

Football.

The academy scouts were coming, weren't they?

If I could wake up. If I could get out of this dead world.

A sudden wail made me jump. I glanced up, holding my breath. A fresh scream tore through the air as the

Darkness slammed into the light again. Motes of dust danced above me.

I had to try something.

The dry ground crunched beneath my feet as I crept toward the edge of camp. The hairs on my arms danced, and my skin felt twice as sensitive. Every breath of wind made me prickle. I glanced over my shoulder, making sure no one was watching.

I hadn't seen anyone go out there since Quinn brought us back. And judging by the stuff they put me through, the film and the lemon balm and all those questions, they didn't want anyone to try.

Up close, the light gave off waves of heat. The thrum of electricity was loud in my ears. The Darkness whooshed and wailed. What would happen if I walked right out?

Jack's thoughts hung just out of reach. I could dive into them . . . I could find out. But if I was going to do this, maybe it would be better not to know. The raw, red marks on my wrists told me I could get hurt here.

I couldn't remember ever feeling pain in a nightmare before. And I'd had some scary ones. Once I fell off the roof of a skyscraper. I'd been chased by monsters and aliens and fought against dragons, but every time anything really bad happened, I always woke up.

Maybe I didn't have to go all the way out.

Maybe it would be enough just to get close . . .

One last glance over my shoulder. No one around.

I walked slowly up to the barrier, held out my hand. It was too big, like the rest of my features when I looked in the mirror at school. I didn't need to see my reflection to know I had blond hair again. Jack's hair and Jack's hands.

I edged my fingers closer to the light. My quickening heart was almost as loud as the screeching storm now. It drummed against my shirt: *thump-thump, thump-thump, thump-thump.*

Whispering broke out all around me, quiet at first, then louder and louder. A vision filled my mind, so sharp and clear. A grave. A headstone marked with a name. *Caroline Smith*. Mum . . .

I couldn't breathe. The whispering came faster and faster. Impish faces appeared in the Darkness, just beyond the barrier of light, beckoning me closer.

Then a yell rang out—a loud, terrible yell.

# 11

Firm hands gripped my shoulders and I cried out in shock.

For a heartbeat I thought it was her. I thought she'd climbed right out of the earth and was dragging me back, back, back through the mud and dust.

"Mum," I choked. "Mum, it's me—"

A man's voice hissed in my ear.

"What do you think you're doing? You could get yourself killed!"

I staggered back, my feet scrabbling on the ground. I clenched my teeth, trying to shrug him off. "I'm just trying to get home!" I tried to sound fierce, but the words came out quiet.

I whirled round, and found myself face to face with Quinn. A badge on his chest displayed the letters lrp. It made me think of police.

"This *is* home, Jack," he said. My shoulders slumped and all the fight, all the energy, drained out of me. I didn't want to be called Jack anymore. Why couldn't they just realize that wasn't my name? This was supposed to be *my* nightmare.

Iris stepped out from behind him, her eyes wide with worry.

"He's . . . he's been acting strangely ever since Cleansing," she said. "He's not . . . you don't think he's . . ." But whatever she was about to say, she couldn't finish.

Quinn gripped my face in his hands. Blue-gray bags spread underneath his eyes, as if he hadn't had a good night's sleep for days.

"No," he said, answering Iris's unasked question. "No, if he was turning, there'd be physical signs by now. Jack . . . what were you thinking? Why would you even go anywhere near it?"

"I . . ." I started to say, but all the argument had leaked out of me, flooding away with the last of my hope. I'd run out of options. I didn't know what to do. "I don't know . . ."

"Do you feel sick at all? Can you still remember the number they gave you in Cleansing?"

"Three hundred and eighty-six," I mumbled. "And . . ." I wondered whether I should tell him about the sick feeling that churned every time I tried to access the part of me that belonged to Jack. His forehead was creased with concern, and Iris was obviously worried if she'd done all this to stop me. "I threw up after they let me out of the chair, but since then I've . . . I've been feeling fine."

"All right," Quinn said, finally stepping back. He turned to Iris. "Sometimes the lemon balm takes a while to kick in. If he's sick any more, come right back to me, and we'll see what we can do. But he looks fine. He's not turning, at any rate."

"Okay," Iris said. She glanced at me, then quickly turned away when she caught me looking.

"As for you," Quinn said, leading me away from the edge of the light, where the Darkness still swirled. "I promised your dad I'd keep you safe, and I can't do that if you go throwing yourself at the storm like that. Go back to your class now, and we'll forget this ever happened. I won't mention it to the Marshal. I won't say a word to anyone. Sound good?"

At the mention of Jack's dad, the whirlwind of thoughts in the back of my mind sped faster, and I gritted my teeth, willing myself not to throw up again.

And the Marshal . . .

As soon as Quinn said his name, an image flashed up. Another face I'd never seen before. Another name I somehow knew.

I looked into Quinn's eyes. He reminded me a little bit of Dad, before the grayness took over his face, before the stress lines made him look older than he was.

I closed my eyes and tried to make sense of everything. It couldn't have been a nightmare, because if it was, I'm sure I would have woken up by now. I couldn't have got knocked out by the bike, because I didn't even hit my head. And it wasn't a hazard I had to warn Dad about, like I first thought, because it was a completely different world. But if it wasn't a nightmare, and I wasn't unconscious, and it wasn't my world, then what was going on?

Those strange changes . . . they began after Dad started writing, didn't they? The first time I noticed the odd features on my face was after our argument. When I jumped into the dead world at school, Dad had been at counseling. And this . . . *Dad was in his study when I left the house!*

A sudden thought hit me. It sounded stupid. Impossible, even. But as soon as I thought it, some part of it made total sense.

What if I wasn't dreaming?

What if . . . what if I'd jumped right into Dad's story?

# 12

*I'm in Dad's story.*

It sounded ridiculous. But the more I thought about it, the more I realized I could be right. I mean . . . the Darkness was a storm, wasn't it? And there was a storm when Dad first started writing again. This place was some dead version of Cambridge. Quinn reminded me of Dad, and Jack . . . I guessed he was a bit like me, because as far as I could tell, he didn't have a mum either. And then there was the lemon balm . . .

But *how*?

That was the thing that didn't make sense. How can anyone just jump into a story? Did it mean this place, this whole camp, was just words on a page? Iris—was she real? Or was she just a character in Dad's head?

Thinking that made the sick feeling squirm inside me again, so I pushed the thoughts away and followed Iris back toward the market. The eyes of all the other kids followed us. Wherever they were going, they didn't stop—just glared as they passed. Was it because I broke the timetable Iris was going on about?

Iris kept glancing at me sideways, as if she expected me to sprout horns at any second.

"I'm not an alien, you know," I said.

"You're freaking me out. I don't care what Quinn said. What *was* that back there?"

I didn't reply, just kept focusing on holding back Jack's thoughts. If they erupted through the fog again, I didn't think I'd be able to avoid throwing up, and if I was sick around Iris . . .

"Jack! Stop ignoring me."

"I'm not ignoring you." I hated myself for telling her. Of course she'd be scared, if her friend didn't know what was going on, if he said he wasn't even from around here. I was so determined to wake up that I didn't stop to think about it.

But if this was Dad's story, then he must be in control of how long I was here for. So I'd better stop acting like Owen, and start being more like Jack.

"It's like Quinn said, the lemon balm is taking a while to kick in. But I'm okay. Really. You don't have to worry."

She shot me a disbelieving look but didn't argue the point any further.

Before long, we arrived at a storm-blackened gateway in a long, eroded wall. I recognized it immediately. I'd been through the real one with Mum. It was one of the entrances to King's College. We paid to look round at the grounds and the chapel. It was beautiful. The buildings dated back hundreds of years, with ancient portraits and wooden carvings designed for King Henry VIII.

There was none of that here. It was like the remains of a castle. The kind where they had to show you paintings to describe what it used to look like, because the crumbled walls made it impossible to tell.

More kids came out through the doorway, most around my age, but some a bit older. I was starting to wonder where all the grown-ups were. I'd only seen a few since we'd got to camp. But I knew better than to ask—I didn't want Iris to panic any more than she had already.

I followed Iris through the entrance. Ahead of us was a wide open space. In my world, it would have revealed magnificent gardens surrounded by high walls. Here there were just burned patches of rubble on the ground and the walls were only partly intact.

A side door led to a stone staircase that went down, down, down into a murky cellar. Lamps flickered on the walls, casting just enough light to see a couple of yards ahead of me. My footsteps echoed on the flagstones, ringing all around.

Then the space opened out, and my jaw dropped.

A row of electric lights hummed gently above us, illuminating a dark arched ceiling and old brick walls. I'd heard about the university cellars. Everyone had. They were supposed to house huge barrels of expensive wine.

This one was converted into a great hall, with cobbled-together beds just visible on the far edges of the room, with scrap curtains dangling around them as if whoever designed them went for all out luxury but gave up halfway. On one side of the room, a sign said girls' dormitories and on the other was boys.

And at the opposite end of the hall—

I'd seen generators before, back in the truck, and in the real world too. Dad had a small one in the garage, and sometimes coach brought one to our school football matches if he knew there was going to be a big crowd, so he could play music and cook food at halftime.

But I'd never seen a generator like this. It was *massive*, and even from here I could make out the knobs and dials, the flashing green lights. Why couldn't I hear it? It was switched on—it must have been, or there wouldn't have been any light to protect the camp. Even the small generators at school rumbled and chugged. The most I could hear now was a low murmur.

It was hard to keep the awe off my face. After seeing how dead the world above was, I never expected anything like this to exist below it. But Iris was watching me carefully as we reached the bottom of the stairs. I cleared my throat and looked over to the right-hand side of the room, so she wouldn't be able to see my reaction.

There was a noticeboard on the wall, covered in crinkled sheets of paper and pinned in place with drawing pins. On either side of it were more TV screens, all show-ing the same thing—footage of families back home in the City, receiving packages of food and drink.

A man appeared onscreen, and the footage shrank as text popped up. It reminded me of charity commercials I'd seen on TV.

". . . Have you ever wanted to be a hero? Now's your chance! As part of Icarus 3, everything you do for our camp will improve life for your families in the City . . ."

". . . Points for you means prizes for them! Don't leave them to suffer while they wait for evacuation . . ."

". . . Remember, the better you do your job, the sooner we can communicate, the faster the evacuation process can begin, and the quicker your family will get their rewards for *your* hard work . . ."

Iris grabbed my arm and pulled me away from the screens.

"We better get changed," she said. "See you in the classroom?"

"Er, yeah," I said. "Yeah, sure."

She headed off to the girls' dormitories. I walked across the hall, passing more kids going the other way. A few of them nodded or waved, but none of them stopped me as I moved through to the dormitory. I froze in the doorway, taking it all in. I didn't know what I'd been expecting, but it wasn't this.

The beds weren't *beds* exactly, just makeshift mattresses covered in fabric. At the foot of each bed was a chest. Most of them were so loaded with junk that the lids couldn't shut, and the objects spilled out over the floor.

There was a name tag on each box, so I worked my way around the room until I found Jack's bed and dug around for some spare clothes. There were T-shirts and trousers, but no shoes.

None of them were clean, exactly, just slightly less dirty than the rags I was wearing. It felt good to get into something dry, but my damp shoes were making me shiver and I couldn't replace them.

I sat down on the bed, taking everything in.

Now that I had a bit of quiet, it was easier to hear myself think.

But as I went back over everything I'd heard since the storm chased us toward camp, I couldn't help feeling uneasy. I was in some kind of weird future, I knew that much. The City was in trouble, and we'd set out trying to find a new home for everyone. And if I'd got it right, somehow our actions here helped our families back home.

Jack's thoughts were still there, buzzing at the back of my mind. I looked up. The room was still empty, and I couldn't see anyone through the doorway. It would be safe, wouldn't it? If I threw up here, no one would see. I took a deep breath to steady my nerves. I needed to know more about the kid inside my head.

I closed my eyes and ventured toward his thoughts.

*I was shut in a cupboard, surrounded by bare walls. I crouched in the corner, hugging my knees, praying they didn't come down here, praying they didn't look—*

*Footsteps on the stairs, booming above my head.*

*My dad's voice, rising, panicked.*

*"There's nothing down there," he said. "Just a cellar. It's where Ayden sleeps—we've only got one room, see, and . . . "*

*They were outside the cupboard now.*

*I held my breath—listening, listening.*

*The handle rattled. The door creaked. They were trying to open it. They were trying to get inside. I rocked again, back and forth, back and forth, not daring to breathe.*

BOOM.

*The door banged open and suddenly there was a wail . . .*

*Two pairs of hands grabbed me, dragging me out . . .*

*Someone crying, "No! Please, not Jack!"*

*Another voice, harsher, hissing, "Be quiet, man!"*

I pulled out of the rush of images, blinking back hot tears. Every breath shuddered on the way in and rattled on the way out. My forehead was slick with sweat.

That had felt so *real* . . . as if . . . as if I'd been there myself.

The afterimage burned whenever I blinked. I could still see it playing out on repeat. Back in the City, officers in the same LRP uniform as Quinn had taken Jack away from his family. But he must have been so young then . . . no more than eight years old. How long had it been since he'd seen them? The fog came back now, and his thoughts cowered behind it, hiding from the pain. The dread he felt still lingered with me.

I had to push through it. I had to know more . . .

I plunged back in, trying to grab the memories as they slipped and slid.

*The thrum of airship propellers filled the air.*

*We were being marched toward the runway, shepherded toward our future on Icarus 3—dozens of other kids and me, with two adults for every ten children in our group. The grown-ups were the leaders, there to train us, teach us, show us how to safeguard the country's history.*

*I turned around desperately, trying to find Dad in the crowd, trying to see Ayden. Thousands of people had gathered to wave us off, their banners held high to cheer us on.*

*There . . . I saw Dad, right up against the barrier they'd put in place to hold everyone back. As soon as I saw him, I knew something was wrong. LRP officers were rushing up to him, barking commands.*

*Dad turned to Ayden and said something, but I was too far away to hear . . .*

*"Dad!" I called, trying to make myself heard above the noise of the propellers.*

*The officers pulled the fence aside, grabbing Dad by the arms. Hardly daring to breathe, I watched as they dragged him away from the crowd.*

*"DAD!"*

*What were they doing? He was a Marshal. They couldn't arrest him . . .*

*But no, they weren't arresting him, I could see that now. They were taking him across the runway, heading toward one of the other ships.*

*"Keep moving!" barked the LRP officer behind me, forcing me back round.*

*"But they've got Dad," I said, desperate to look back again, desperate to see.*

"Anyone caught sheltering duplicates is joining them on their mission," the LRP officer said.

"What? No! Dad! Get off me . . . DAD!" I called, trying to fight my way free.

He did look up then, just before he reached the ramp leading up to the Icarus 1 airship, a hundred yards away. For a heartbeat, everything seemed to freeze. He waved at me, but before I could wave back, the moment passed and he was shoved up onto the deck and lost from sight.

# 13

I hadn't thrown up this time, but seeing Jack's memories left me feeling hollow and weak. Jack's dad wasn't in the City at all—he'd been taken, just like us, taken to Icarus 1, to fly off who knew where. I had no idea if he was alive or dead.

I didn't dare dive back into the fog after that. It was too hard. I was still shaking from the effort. All of a sudden I felt bad for even trying. After the first time, I could tell Jack was trying to battle me off. He didn't want to relive those memories, and I made him.

I sat there for a few more minutes, until I was sure I wasn't going to puke. Then, when I felt I could stand again, I worked my way out into the hall.

It was eerily empty now. The TVs on the wall had been switched off, the only sound the gentle hum of the generator on my left. Between the generator and the girls' dormitories, there was another door leading to a corridor. Above it, a sign read classrooms.

On my way there, I passed the noticeboard again. *The timetable*, I realized, as I got closer. Each day was set out in blocks. Class, Farming, Hunting, and Stormwalking, set out in different orders for different people.

This must have been what all the kids were rushing around doing. They were being put to work. But why kids? It couldn't just be that we were duplicates. I headed through the door to the classrooms, my mind racing furiously.

If this place was supposed to help save the City, I didn't understand why they'd brought so many children. Surely an adult would make a better Farmer than me?

More lights along the ceiling lit the way ahead and picked out three doors on either side of the corridor— six classrooms in total. I dried my palms on my trousers, then walked to the door marked 3B. The sign outside read michelle cloud, pre-darkness history and literature.

I couldn't stand around forever. I opened the door.

"Ah, Jack," said the teacher, and I was relieved to see an adult. "I was wondering where you were." Her clothes were worn down, like everyone else's I'd seen here, but they weren't anywhere near as bad as mine.

"Sorry," I muttered, squelching into the room and wishing I'd managed to find some different shoes. "I just had a bit of a . . . um . . . problem."

"Not to worry. Take a seat quickly. We're studying some exciting objects today."

I looked round the room. You could tell someone had tried to clean it up. The walls were washed, and the paint was less patchy. The roof was whole and there was no ivy growing through it.

There were three rows of tables laid out, scrawled over and covered with black burn marks, even worse than the desks in the Science block at school. None of the chairs matched.

I found a seat at the back, next to Iris. I noticed her checking on me as I turned to the board.

"Today we're focusing on history," Mrs. Cloud said.

She pressed a button, and a large screen flashed on at the head of the class, just like the one they used back in Cleansing. And for the first time I realized what was odd about it, just like the other one: it didn't have any power cables.

"What I'd like you to look at," Mrs. Cloud said, bringing up an image of some small plastic disks, "is something the pre-Darks called tiddlywinks. I have some examples here, scavenged by Iris—" Mrs. Cloud smiled at Iris; she blushed and looked away—"and very kindly donated for the lesson. I'll pass them round so you can hold them in a minute."

Mrs. Cloud held up one of the disks between forefinger and thumb.

"Does anyone know what they might have been used for?"

One of the boys in the front row thrust his hand up. "Er, as decoration?" he said. "You could put it on the wall or something. Like a painting, but small and shimmery."

"You could, Alex, yes. But I'm afraid you're not quite right."

"Is it part of a necklace?" said another boy—and I realized it was Dillon, who I'd been out in the storm with.

"It could be, couldn't it?" the teacher said, holding the piece of plastic below her neck. "But I'm looking for something else, something a little more academic."

Iris held her hand in the air. "I think I've seen them in *Understanding the Pre-Dark World*," she said. "It's a sort of counting system, isn't it?"

"Indeed," Mrs. Cloud said. She turned to face the screen, and pressed a button. An animation played, showing some kids doing math with them.

"As we understand it, tiddlywinks were quite a popular teaching tool, although evidently not as dominant as some of the other methods we've studied—"

My mouth dropped open. I couldn't stop a laugh escaping.

"Is everything okay, Jack?" Mrs. Cloud said.

I clamped my mouth shut and looked round at the class. Everyone was staring at me. My neck tingled, and suddenly I didn't know what to say.

I had thought about the future a lot. Everyone did, I guessed. You did it all the time, just watching things like *Star Wars* or *Iron Man*. But whenever you thought of the future, you imagined flying cars and laser guns and people curing all the diseases with their amazing technology.

Some of the technology here was pretty impressive, like the generator that was a million times quieter than the one in the equipment room at school, and the way none of their TVs needed cables.

But I never thought anyone would forget stuff about the past.

"Er," I said, trying to think of the best way to phrase it. "Sorry, it's just . . . well, I don't think that's what tiddly-winks were used for."

"There are some very learned Scholars who would disagree with you," Mrs. Cloud said, frowning.

Out of the corner of my eye I saw Iris staring at me, and suddenly guilt gnawed at my insides. I mean, if this was a story then it didn't really matter what they thought, did it? They were just in Dad's imagination.

"What do you think they were used for, if not for math?"

"For fun?" I said.

"I'm sorry?"

"For fun. It's a game. You ping them into a cup."

Mrs. Cloud burst out laughing, along with the rest of the class. I felt my cheeks growing hot. "A fine notion," she said, "but I think we'll go with the original interpretation in this case."

For the rest of the lesson, I didn't say anything. Not even when she unveiled an old, dirt-covered phone charger and started talking about its benefits as a weapon. Partly because I didn't want to get laughed at again. But also because something told me it would be safer to keep quiet. If they figured out I wasn't from around here, who knew what they'd do?

# 14

"Why did you say that?" Iris said.

She was waiting for me outside the classroom.

I paused in the doorway. The only sound was the low hum of the lights above us, casting their electric glow throughout the corridor.

"Because it's true," I said.

Even if I wanted to, I wouldn't have been able to access Jack's thoughts. They were still hiding, still reeling from the memory. It was impossible to get close to them.

"You've never said anything like that before. You were there when I found them. Why didn't you mention it then?"

"Iris . . ."

How could I tell her without freaking her out? I couldn't exactly just say, "You're a character in a story," could I? I couldn't just come out with it. "Oh, none of this is real. I'll jump home soon and have school and a football match against Westfield and, when I do, you'll be gone."

Because if I did, she'd go straight back to Quinn.

And because standing here in front of her felt real. The heat of her glare was just as real as it would be in real life. The scuffing noise she made twisting her foot sounded just as real too. But I couldn't just say nothing. I had to find a way of getting home, and some part of me—some part of Jack, maybe—trusted her. Maybe she could help . . .

"This . . . this isn't my world," I said.

"You're my friend," she said, pulling me into a corner. "I've known you for years. I know Quinn said you weren't turning, but you're going crazy or *something*. There *is* no other world. This is it. It's just us. And, if we're lucky, the City, if we can get through to them before it's too late."

I didn't want to argue, I just wanted her to understand. "Maybe I am going crazy. But I'm telling you the truth. I might be in Jack's body, but I'm not Jack. I don't know about any of this stuff. Hunting, LRP . . . That robot called us Stormwalkers, and I don't even want to know what that means."

Iris stared at me, her face pale. "I don't want you to turn Dreamless," she said in a quiet, croaky voice that made her sound much younger than she looked. "Please, we can go to the Marshal—he knows all about the mind—"

"Jack's still here," I said quickly. "I can see his life, like I'm watching it on TV. Or, I could, at least, until a few minutes ago. I know all about his dad and Ayden. Jack's still here. It's just . . . I'm here too."

"That's ridiculous," Iris said. At the mention of Ayden's name, she seemed to relax a little, but she was still watching me warily. "It's impossible."

"Tell me about it! Try waking up in the future, trapped in a world you don't belong in."

"The . . . the future?" she said. She tugged a strand of hair, twisting it round her fingers. She shook her head, slowly at first, then more vigorously. "I don't believe you."

"Then let me show you!" I balled my fists in frustration, rocking back and forth on my heels. Why couldn't she see? "Let me prove it somehow—I don't know . . . just . . . you have to believe me."

I didn't know why I cared so much. When I *did* get back, I'd never see her again. Maybe it was part of Jack's bond seeping into my mind, or maybe it was the fire in her eyes, her outright refusal to see it. It felt like I had a giant weight hanging in my chest, and if I could just get her to see the truth, it would dissolve.

"You're saying you're a pre-Dark? You expect me to believe that?"

"Yes!" I said, before realizing that, actually, that wasn't what I'd meant at all. "I mean, maybe, I don't know. I'm saying that where I'm from, it's not even 2024 yet, and according to that video I saw in Cleansing, 2024 is way, *way* in the past here."

Iris was still shaking her head. "You know how much I love history. This isn't funny."

"I'm not trying to be funny. There must be a way for me to prove it."

The silence stretched out between us. At the far end of the corridor, the door opened and a new group of kids came in, talking over one another.

"Follow me," Iris said, lowering her voice.

She led me back into the main hall, then through the arch to the girls' dorms. A few people rushed back past us, their arms full of something that glimmered a dozen different colors in the light.

"Are they bottle caps?" I asked.

Iris glanced sideways at me. I was supposed to know stuff like this, wasn't I? If I was Jack, he'd know what was happening. I tried to access his thoughts again, but they hung out of reach.

"You're going to go very hungry if you've forgotten about caps too," she said, narrowing her eyes at me. She still didn't believe me, did she? She still thought I was making it all up . . .

"They're for food?" I said.

There were more questions bubbling in my mind, but I didn't ask them, even though I wanted to find out what scraps of metal had to do with food.

*Food . . .*

My stomach grumbled. How long had it been since I last ate?

"I'll check no one's around," Iris said, when we arrived at the door. "Everyone should be in the square by now, but you never know."

She poked her head inside, then hissed for me to follow her.

The walls were bare. The smell of dust clung to the air. There was a table in the corner covered in junk. More rubbish spilled out from under one of the beds, and, I realized, seeing the name badge, it must have all belonged to her. Old clocks and dusty books, playing cards and photo frames. The kind of stuff you'd find in charity shops round town.

"I want you to look at something," Iris said. She rummaged under her bed. "If you really are a pre-Dark, you'll know all about it."

"What is all this?"

Iris shook her head in disbelief.

"The most important stuff in the world. When we go Hunting, we're supposed to bring back the really important things we find, like gasoline or food or whatever. But if I can, I collect antiques. With these things, I get to hold a piece of history. If I close my eyes, I can almost imagine I'm there." She emerged with something in her hands. It was so heavily rusted that at first I couldn't tell what it was. Flakes of copper-colored metal crumbled away beneath her fingers. She held it out to me, cradling it in her hands like a delicate flower. "Do you remember when we found this?"

My eyes drifted from her face to the object and back. Even though it was in bad shape, I could tell what it was. Dad had one at home from when he was a kid. He used to try to get me to play with it when I'd spent too long on the PlayStation.

"It's a Slinky," I said.

"A slinky," she repeated slowly, as if the letters were puzzle pieces that didn't fit together. I'd never really thought about the word *slinky* before, but the way she said it made it sound funny. "I don't know where you're getting all this from. First the tiddlywinks, now this. Jack, please tell me you remember when we found it. That crater. The way you fought off the Dreamless with it . . ."

She flung the metal rings from her hands so they rattled and clinked on the floor. Then she flicked her wrist and the slinky whipped back up. Her fingers had turned red-brown where the rust rubbed off.

She handed me the Slinky.

"Say you remember," she said, a pleading tone in her voice now.

If I could get through to Jack's thoughts, maybe I'd be able to give her the answer she wanted. But the more I tried to reach them, the more they slipped away.

"I . . . used a Slinky as a weapon?"

"It's . . . it's not a weapon?"

"Not really," I said, trying to think of a way to say it without seeming rude. "It's just a toy."

She frowned. I could almost see her brain working: trying to figure out how a bunch of metal rings could ever be a toy.

"A toy," she repeated.

"I know it sounds weird."

"Weird doesn't even begin to cover it," she said.

"Look, I'm sorry. I already tried to tell you, all this is new to me. I don't even know what a . . . what a *Dreamless* is."

Iris's eyes widened, then narrowed to slits. "Yeah, well, maybe it's best that way."

She grabbed the Slinky and marched back toward the door.

"Does that mean you believe me?" I called after her.

"No," she said. "It means I'm going to talk to Quinn. This is *really* bad, Jack."

She vanished, and, pausing just for a moment to take in all the rubbish—all the objects she obviously considered treasure—I ran after her.


The market square was filled with children, kids my age and older, swapping junk for bottle caps and scoffing strange-looking food. A sweet, buttery smell filled the air and my stomach grumbled again.

"Iris . . ." I started, chasing after her.

"Where do you live?" she said, turning on me and shoving me hard in the chest. "If you really are a pre-Dark, where do you live?"

"Well . . . here," I said. "In Cambridge."

"Cambridge?"

"That's what this place is called, back where I'm from. It's not called that here?"

She shook her head. "I don't know what it's called. Maybe it was part of the City once, but not anymore. We just call it the camp."

Iris was quiet for a while. I looked around for any sign of adults, and there were a few, dotted here and there, but even the people behind the stalls were quite young, maybe eighteen or nineteen.

"They're retired Stormwalkers," she said, reading the expression on my face. The way she looked at me, I could tell she still didn't believe me about not being Jack, but there was something else there too. Tiredness, maybe. If she thought I was playing a game, she'd got bored of it.

"*Retired?* They look like they should still be in school."

"They are," she said. "I mean, they still go to class with the Scholars. They just don't go out into the storm anymore. It—" she hesitated, choosing the right words— "acts differently around younger kids. It feeds on fear, and I guess as you get older you've got more to be scared of. You can't Stormwalk once you hit eighteen. You have to find other jobs. That's why they use us—kids, I mean. I mean, yeah, we're duplicates, so we're expendable, I guess. But it's safer for us out there, if you can call it safe at all."

*Nice*, I thought. They took us away when we were eight, used us for the most dangerous job left on the planet, and then just like that we were supposed to sell weird *Star Wars* food to the rest of the camp. I wondered what life was like back in the City . . . could it really be so bad that they needed us to go through this?

"Are there bookshops?" Iris said suddenly.

"What?"

"Back in . . . what did you call it? Cambridge?"

"Loads. With walls piled high with books." She stared off into the distance. Maybe she was finally starting to believe me! "Do . . . do you like reading?"

She scowled at me, and marched off again. I stood there for a moment, wondering what I'd done wrong, then quickly chased after her. I didn't want to lose the only friend I had in this place. Well . . . I had Quinn, I guessed, but Iris was different. I felt like I'd known her all my life.

And I had, hadn't I? If I was Jack . . . if Jack was me . . . I'd known her for years.

"Sorry! Iris, I'm sorry—I know that—of course I know that. It's just, if I try to dive into the memories . . ." I trailed off. I couldn't let her know it made me feel ill. It would only worry her more.

"Do you have any idea how ridiculous this is?" she said.

"I know. Just . . . please, don't take me back to Cleansing, or . . . or any of that stuff. You don't have to worry about me. Just . . . give me some time."

With a pang, it dawned on me how similar to Dad I sounded. Did I say that on my own, or was it his writing that made it happen?

Iris turned on me, and I jumped back in case she thumped me again. "This is what I don't get. If you *were* turning Dreamless, there would be physical signs by now. Quinn was right."

"I'm still trying to figure this out too. But I'm telling you the truth."

I couldn't blame her for not believing me. If I were in her place, I'd probably be the same.

Her eyes locked onto mine, watering at the edges. Then she blinked and turned away.

She strode up to the nearest table, muttering and shaking her head. The man behind the stall had a grizzled, stubbly face and a gap in his teeth when he smiled. "What you got, love?"

Iris dropped the Slinky on the table.

She was giving it up after telling me how much all her collection meant to her?

"Iris—"

"It's fine," she said.

The man picked it up and eyeballed it, watching as flecks of rust crumbled off.

"Not much here. About two caps' worth, I reckon."

"Two caps?" Iris scoffed. She glanced at me quickly before saying, "It's a pre-Dark weapon. Deadly in the right hands."

"We don't need weapons, love. Not this kind. Most I can do with this is melt it down. Two caps or nothing."

She hesitated, her cheeks reddening, then held out her hand to catch the caps—basic, unmarked bottle tops, just like the ones that piled up on the counter when Dad drank his beers.

"Still here?" she said to me, as she walked round to the food stall.

"I don't know what to say . . ."

But Iris wasn't listening.

"Two caps," she muttered under her breath. "We won't be able to get much. What?" she said, noticing the look on my face.

"Nothing—it's just . . ."

I was going to say it was funny seeing a kid act like this. She'd have probably only been in Year 8 at school, but here she was haggling at market stalls like it was the easiest thing in the world.

A spark of hunger flickered inside me again, and I clutched my stomach. But as soon as I saw what was laid out on the table, any thought of devouring a massive meal vanished. There was no pizza or bacon or chicken. There weren't even any sandwiches.

Set out in rows were . . .

Well, I wasn't really sure what they were. They were round, like fishcakes, but bright yellow. They looked disgusting.

"Fresh corn rounds," the vendor said. "One cap a pair."

Iris handed over the caps, but even though my stomach felt as empty as it had ever been, the thought of eating those corn rounds almost made me gag.

"They're not that bad," Iris said, nibbling cautiously at the edge of hers. It crumbled like shortbread, and she had to eat the rest quickly before it fell apart.

Deciding that the best thing to do was get it over with as quickly as possible, I took a bite and chewed. The outside was crispy and peppery, but the inside tasted like powdered mashed potatoes. I thought back to all the fast food I'd eaten with Dad before that homemade burger the other day and promised never to moan about takeout again.

"Thanks," I said, when I'd choked both of them down.

"You can buy dinner tomorrow," she said.

"I . . . I don't know how. I mean, I don't have any caps or anything. I don't even know how you get them."

She gave me that look again, like I was an alien or something.

"What?"

"I don't know," she said. "It's like you *are* Jack, but you're not."

I was about to say that that was what I'd been trying to tell her all along, when a robot scooted by, its blue-white dome flashing like a TV screen again.

"All classes report to the . . . MAIN HALL," it said. "The . . . STORMWALKING . . . is about to begin."

# 15

*Stormwalking!*

I remembered seeing it in the video at Cleansing, and Iris had mentioned it since. It had been there in Jack's memories too, when I was trying to find out more about him. I didn't get to see much of it before the fog rose up, but just hearing the word made icicles of cold prod at my insides. After getting so close to the Darkness twice already, I wasn't ready to go right back out into it.

Iris and I filed into the hall once more, joining the other Stormwalkers filling up the vast room. Most of the floor space was packed with kids, but there were a few grown-ups dotted around. I recognized the women who had quizzed me after Cleansing hanging around at the edge of the group and Mrs. Cloud whispering with a tall, gray-haired man. Quinn entered, and with him came other officers in the same uniform, lrp emblazoned on their chests. Beside them was someone I hadn't seen before.

No—

I *had* seen him before.

He was the man from the video footage.

The man in the commercials.

*The Marshal*, came a thought in my head.

He had thin white hair, and a round belly pushed up against his shirt. His clothes were cleaner than the stuff everyone else wore. He stood before the group and when it looked as though everyone had gathered, he cleared his throat and held up his hands.

You could feel the buzz in the room now. Questions erupted in my mind, but the crowd had separated me from Iris.

"Welcome, everyone, to another Stormwalking!"

A huge cheer rang out, echoing off the walls.

"Ever since we set off from the City, looking for a place to live, a place to expand, a place to *thrive*, we have been on a very important mission: to save the human race. Now that we have established camp, that mission has never been more important.

"Hope! That is what we set out to find. That is what we must protect. That is what we must relay to the City, to our families, our friends, to all those left behind. They have no space to live. We do. But that *storm*," he said, wagging a finger at the ceiling, "is separating us from our loved ones.

"Every day, through your good work, the Lights, Radio, and Patrol team tries to send word to them.

Every day they listen out for word from our brothers and sisters in Icarus 1 and 2, to see if they have had any luck breaking through." He paused to shake his head, and sighed heavily. "Alas, there is still no response— from the other camps, *or* the City. It's troubling, yes, of course it's troubling, but now is not the time to dwell on misfortune. If the other Icarus teams have fallen to the Darkness, it only makes our job more important.

"Now that we have found somewhere for our families to live and breathe and expand, we must make contact with the City. The storm makes it tough to communicate. You've seen how short the daylight pockets are, and they're different across the country. But you, dear Stormwalkers, are stronger than the storm—I know you are. The City needs us. We cannot fail. We are Icarus 3, and we *will* save them. Seth?" the Marshal called, and the crowd parted, leaving a lone figure standing in the middle of the crowd. "Let the Stormwalking commence!"

I stepped back, standing on tiptoes, trying to see what was happening. A booming rumble echoed round the cellar and a circle of green lights flashed in the shadows at the back of the room, behind the Marshal. There was a *hiss* and a *clunk*, and the lights rotated. A door opened where the lights had been, revealing a tunnel that stretched out into the distance and disappeared in shadow.

A circle of space had opened up in the crowd now, and standing there was a boy unlike anyone I'd seen in camp so far. He wasn't dressed in dirty old clothes, like the rest of us. He wore a jet-black top with matching trousers. On his shoulders and chest gleamed neon-bright lights, like reflectors on a bike, but much brighter.

Seth stared round at us, the lights dancing like fire in his eyes.

"We'll be going in groups of four," he said. "As I call your name, come and collect your equipment. There are fresh meadows near the top of tower hill, the whispering rock, and the scarlands. Start there, and fan out, just like normal. Okay, Cora! You're up."

A tall, dark-haired girl moved through the crowd. Seth grabbed a handful of jackets from the tunnel, each of them riddled with lights, like the top he was wearing, and handed one of them to her.

"Anja!"

I tried to move in for a closer look as the next girl collected her gear, but the hall was thick with bodies. I ducked elbows and shimmied between shoulders. Bright lights gleamed along Anja's shoulders, arms and body as she fastened the jacket over her clothes.

"Luke," called Seth, "Tyler . . . Dillon . . . Iris . . . *Jack*."

I stared around the room. People clapped my shoulders, shoved me forward, buffeted me toward the open gap. I felt the Marshal's eyes burning into me as I made my way to the center of the ring and took the suit from Seth.

Up close, the lights were so bright that purple splotches smudged across my vision when I blinked. There was a slimline compartment on the back of the jacket, with a zipper that ran all around it.

"For the glowroot," Iris whispered, when she saw me looking. "It protects it. Keeps it safe."

"Glowroot," I whispered. I remembered seeing it in Jack's thoughts, back in Cleansing.

"It's this weed that grows only in Darkness," she explained. "It glows."

"I sort of guessed that much."

"Nothing can grow in the Darkness. You've seen the food we have to eat. But somehow the glowroot does. The Darkness can't get close to it. We've studied it for years, even back in the City, trying to understand it. The Marshals figured out how to turn it into energy. That's how the generators run. The illuminators too," she added, tapping the lights on her suit. "They run out pretty quickly though, so we have to keep reloading them."

"What does it look like?"

"You'll know when you see it," she said, smirking.

The jackets were skintight, like the cold gear you could get for sport back in the real world. I slipped mine over my clothes, then turned to Iris. But before I could ask her anything, Seth strode over. He'd handed out all the equipment.

"You three are with me," he said to Iris, me, and the boy called Tyler, who looked older than a lot of the others. He had a square jaw and short, dark hair. If they'd had rugby here, he'd totally be a rugby player. "There's a new route I'd like to try out."

\* \* \*

Cold. That was the first thing that hit me.

Cutting through the fabric of my clothes—

Biting down to my bones—

As the door boomed shut behind us and the noise of camp cut off, screeches and shrieks rang out in the distance. I didn't have to be an A-star student to know what we were going to find at the end of the tunnel . . .

"Stay close," Seth said.

He stepped forward, and a light hummed on above us.

Another flickered into life with every step—motion-sensitive lamps, lighting the path ahead. The tunnel walls dripped as we passed. The air was thick and damp. We shuffled forward, feet scuffing on the flagstones, and I realized I was holding my breath. Other Stormwalkers rushed past, eager to get out into the Darkness, or maybe eager to get back into the safety of the light.

"What is it?" Iris said, dropping back to walk with me. "Your face is all scrunched up. You're not going to have to touch it, if that's what you're worried about. Hopefully, anyway."

"I'm not worried about that," I said, even though I was, I definitely was, because I'd felt what happened if it got too close, and even though we had illuminators this time, it felt way too dangerous going out like this.

Seth and Tyler were walking quickly ahead of us. The Darkness was so loud now that I didn't think they'd be able to hear us.

"Keep up," Seth barked. "We can't afford to separate here."

Ahead of us now was a pile of rubble where the roof had caved in, blocking the route ahead. There was a ragged hole above us, and a few yards above that . . .

I stepped back instinctively.

It flashed past in a whirling rush, as black as midnight and shot through with crackling purple, bubbling up and bursting in the shape of a hundred sneering faces . . .

The Darkness.

"Everyone ready?" Seth said. "Tyler, watch our backs. Keep an eye out for anything I miss. I know the tower's not that far, but we don't know how different the route is yet. Iris, Jack—follow me." He darted out, sending shards of stone tinkling back down into the light.

I thought the screeching in camp was loud, but it wasn't. Not compared to this. The second Seth's illuminators hit the open air, the Darkness peeled back as if in agony and the noise was unbearable.

Tyler had already scrambled up one way. Iris clambered out the other, following Seth. I took a deep breath and chased after them. As soon as I emerged, the Darkness bolted down from the heavens. Long tendrils lashed out, whipping at my face.

*It's just a storm*, I told myself, hammering the thought home.

*It's just a storm and this is just a story and soon enough you'll be home, chatting with Dad and Danny and—*

The Darkness screamed again and I ducked as it whooshed over my head.

All around me clicks rang out, like thousands of insects snapping their pincers at once. I gulped the cold air, looking desperately for Iris and Seth, every breath full of white-hot needles stabbing my insides.

*There!*

In the distance, the swirl of illuminators. I bolted after them, not daring to look back. A drawn-out scream split the air, sending electric tingles up and down the back of my neck.

"Jack!" Iris called. "Come on!"

I raced on and caught them as they skidded down the muddy bank to the river. The water trickled peacefully alongside us, untouched by the storm. Our illuminators reflected and shimmered on the surface.

"Where now?" I yelled, trying to make myself heard above the ear-splitting noise.

"There! I can see one." Seth followed the curve of the river with his finger. In the distance, I could just make out a pool of ethereal light, like luminescent jellyfish sunbathing on the bank.

"A meadow," Iris said, squinting through the gloom.

We walked together along the river's edge—the Darkness raging above us, but never getting too close. But before we even got to the glowing green carpet of light, it was clear that something was wrong.

"No," Seth said, barely audible above the noise.

Petals and plants were strewn across the mud, trodden in and crumpled. The ghostly green light came off their leaves, and pooled around them like blood on the earth.

I didn't know what it was meant to look like, but I guessed not this.

"What's happened?" Tyler wheezed.

"The whole meadow's crushed," Iris said, crouching over the flowers. She picked up a petal and rubbed it between her fingers. The green light spread over her skin. She looked as if she'd dipped her hand in glow-in-the-dark paint.

I squinted into the distance. The meadow stretched off into the blackness, but nearly every flower was dead.

"What did this?" I said. "I thought glowroot was safe from the storm."

Tyler nudged an upturned plant with the toe of his shoe. "It wasn't the storm . . ."

As if to reinforce his point, a noise rumbled to the west—deep, low, growling.

"What was that?" Iris said.

"I don't know," Seth muttered, "but we need to move. We've got to find another patch." He pointed again, and I could just make out the dark shape of the radio tower silhouetted against the swirling storm. It was high on a hill, the tallest thing around for miles. "That's where we take up the road. If we're lucky, we can follow the lights until—"

Another roar, much closer this time.

Something lunged out of the gloom and Tyler fell, stumbling back. One of his illuminators cracked, and the light leaked out, pooling on the floor like the dead glowroot.

"Dreamless!" Seth cried.

My heart in my throat, I stared at the thing as it lurched out of the gloom. It wasn't a man, although it was man shaped. Its skin was pasty, rippled with burn marks. In the illuminator light bouncing off its face, I could see its mouth frothing. It snorted and sprang at us again even as the Darkness renewed its frenzied shrieking and sped down, down, down, getting too close to us, getting way too close—

A scream ripped the air all around me and at first I thought it was the Darkness, but then I realized my mouth hung open and my lungs burned, and the sound, the long, drawn-out sound, was coming from me.

I forced my mouth shut and swallowed to ease my throat. My legs buckled and I fell to the ground, every part of my body wracked with stabbing pain.

But that wasn't the worst part.

The worst part was in my head. I could see it, like a distant photo getting closer and closer.

*No, don't think about it. Don't think about it.*

But I couldn't stop it. The memory was there now. It was in my head and I couldn't get rid of it. I was in a park, surrounded by green trees. The sun was high in the sky and the birds were singing and I could hear the gentle murmur of the River Cam.

*No . . .*

It used to be a happy place. We fed the ducks all the time. We ripped up bread and stuffed it in a sandwich bag and waited for them to waddle over.

But not this time.

I knew what was coming. I shook my head, trying to fight it, but I couldn't.

Mum appeared out of the fog, walking alongside me . . .

*I've got something I need to tell you*, she said. I got really excited. I thought we were going to get sweets. I thought she was going to say, "Let's go to the shop." But when she turned toward me, she didn't say that at all.

She was crying.

We were supposed to be having fun but she turned to me with wobbling lips and wet cheeks and I didn't understand why.

*I'm afraid . . .* she said, *I'm afraid it's . . . it's bad news.*

And that was when the tears stopped trickling down her cheeks and flooded more freely. She didn't even try to wipe them away. She just cried and cried.

*I wish I didn't have to tell you this. But, darling, I've got . . . I've got—*

*LA-LA-LA.*

*Stop thinking about it, stop thinking about it, stop thinking about it.*

Something gripped my ankle. I struggled against it. I twisted and turned, yelped and kicked out, but instead of frothy snarling I was met with—

"Ow!"

The dry earth scratched my skin as I got dragged back, back into the meadow-light. When I looked up, it wasn't a Dreamless leering down at me. The adrenaline had worn off now, and the pain kicked in again. I clenched my eyes tight shut, but my head still burned.

Iris held me steady, wafting one of her arms through the air above us, sending illuminator-light stabbing up into the sky. Seth rushed over, and pushed us in the direction of the tunnel.

"Run!" he yelled. "Get back to the camp!"

He turned and helped Tyler to his feet, staggering under his weight.

The Darkness peeled away, chittering madly, but the Dreamless was still close—I could smell it. A dank smell. A putrid smell, like rotten fish.

The storm whirled above us, getting closer and closer, testing the protection of the ethereal light. And as it did, something rang in my ears. Not the screeching. It was Mum's voice, calling out, whispering—

*"Owen,"* she said.

*"I've got . . . I've got leukemia."*

"Go!" Seth yelled again.

Tyler regained his footing. He broke away, dashing toward the tunnel just as another roar rumbled somewhere nearby. With every ounce of strength I could summon, I turned and ran, pulse pounding, back through the storm toward camp.

# 16

A car horn blared.

There was a flash of blinding light. Adrenaline surged through me and I scrambled out of the road just as the car thundered past.

I fell to my knees and closed my eyes, trying to shut everything out.

*Where am I? Am I still in the story?*

All my thoughts clouded together. When you were on your own, it was easy to hear yourself in your mind. But right then it wasn't just myself I heard. There was another voice too. Growing smaller and smaller all the time, but definitely there in the back of my mind.

Images flashed up, memories of the dead world, and at first it was impossible to find *me*, to find my name and my memories and my life. I tried to fight through the noise.

And something rose up out of the jumbled rush . . .

The West Essex Rovers. We played them in the school cup last year and I got hacked on the edge of the box. I took the free kick, but I was so worked up that the shot went wide. For the rest of the game, the kid who fouled me kept jeering. I wanted to shut him up by playing the best I could, but every time I tried to do something good I messed up. I just got worse and worse. It was like I was playing in quicksand.

That was how this felt. Like there was nothing I could do. Like I was drowning.

"Are you all right, mate?" said a voice beside me.

I jumped in surprise, staggering back into a wall—

My head rang. I clutched my stomach, trying not to throw up. I checked my hands. They were mine again. I could tell by my little finger. It was crooked where it'd got broken by a cricket ball in PE.

"You okay?" said the voice again. A boy's voice.

"Yeah," I mumbled, glancing across at him. He had school uniform on, but wasn't the same as mine. We were at a bus stop, but there was no name on the sign, just a number. "Where are we?"

"Victoria Road," he said.

"What?" That was forty minutes from my house. Unless I ran. And my legs were too weak for that. My head pounded. My palms were clammy with sweat. *How did I get here?* I kept thinking about the storm, about us running out into it. We hadn't got very far at all. We were supposed to get glowroot for the generators in camp. We were supposed to help power the radio tower. But we didn't get anything. And Mum's voice . . . I shivered just thinking about it.

"Do you think you should go to the doctor or something?"

"No. No, I'm okay."

Even though I wasn't okay. I was far, far from okay. I was miles away from home, and I had no idea how I got there. I leaned against the wall to hide my buckling knees. I tried to think back to what I was doing before I jumped into the dead world, but my thoughts flickered and flashed and popped before I could get to them.

Home. I needed to get home.

I felt for my wallet, but there was only thirty-five pence in there, and there was no way I'd be able to get a bus with that. I dug out my phone and sent a text to Danny.

Can you bike to Victoria Road?

On a bike, the journey's nothing. He'd be here in ten minutes max, and I could hitch a ride home on the back. I didn't have to wait long for a reply.

Sod off.

*What?* I knew it was out of the blue, but if he didn't want to give me a ride, he only had to say so. Danny was always smiling, always cracking jokes. He'd never replied to me like that before.

Then I noticed the messages above mine. There were loads of them, all from Danny.

Where are you?
Smithy???
Thought you'd like to know we lost. Thanks, mate.

For a second I stood there frowning. What was he going on about? Then it hit me—

No . . .

"What day is it today?" I asked. My stomach writhed again but for a different reason.

"Wednesday." The boy gave me the kind of look Mrs. Laird gave you when you said you'd forgotten your homework.

"Wednesday? How can it be Wednesday?"

If it was Wednesday, then—

I'd missed the game.

Westfield. We were supposed to play them today.

"Look," said the boy again, the same worried expression on his face. "Are you sure you're okay? I don't mind going to the doctor's with you if you want? It's just round the corner."

"I'm fine," I snapped.

But right away I felt bad, because it wasn't his fault. He hadn't done anything.

*What am I going to say to Danny?* I thought.

*What am I going to say to Dad?*

Because if I'd missed the football, then I'd missed four days of school as well. I checked the time on my phone.

The numbers flashed up: 7:30. The sudden panic made my stomach churn. It was half past seven on Wednesday evening, and the last thing I remembered . . .

The last thing I remembered was going out on Friday morning.

# 17

The smell was thick in the air before I got to the kitchen. Garlic and mushrooms and cheese. I'd never felt so hungry before. It felt as if a cave had opened up inside my stomach, stretching wider and wider. I could even have eaten a plateful of those corn rounds.

"Owen!" Dad said, blinking when he saw me in the hall. "Sorry—I just cooked for myself. I thought . . ." He shook his head, rubbed his hair. "I thought you were at Danny's. That's odd. Why wouldn't I make anything for you?"

He stared at his food as if expecting to find answers in it.

I waited in the doorway, staring at him. Didn't he care? I'd missed six whole days of my life, doing what? Either I'd vanished from this world completely, or else I'd been zoned out somewhere. But zoned out for days on end?

Surely he would have called the police. Someone would have noticed. Wouldn't they?

"It's okay," I said, just to break the silence. "I'll grab something from the fridge."

"No." Dad shook himself. "No, we'll share this. Gives us more space for dessert."

He winked, then gestured to the kitchen table. I sat down as he split the meal over two plates. My stomach rumbled loudly, but even louder than that were the questions clamoring in my mind. I always told Dad when I was going over to Danny's, and I definitely hadn't mentioned it the other day. Why would he think I'd gone over there?

"Did anyone from school ring?" I asked, watching him carefully.

He shrugged. He scratched the stubble on his chin.

"No," he said. "I would have heard. I've been in the study all day. Been writing. The words are flowing, Owen. The story's working."

"That's great," I said, and I really meant it, but I was distracted by a million more questions. Mrs. Willoughby always rang if you weren't there. If you didn't let her know you were going to be absent by nine o'clock, she'd keep ringing home until she had proof that you were ill. But she hadn't called. No one at school had.

A thought bubbled up in the back of my mind.

"What did we do yesterday?" I asked.

Dad frowned. He had been about to eat a forkful of food, but it hung there now, hovering a couple of inches from his mouth. "What do you mean?" he said.

"My mind's gone blank," I said. "I'm just trying to remember."

"Well, you went to school, and when you got back . . ."

"When I got back, what?" I said.

"You . . . er . . ." He chewed his lips, frowning. He rubbed the top of his head, where his hair was getting thinner, and scratched his chin. "You know what? My mind's gone blank too. Would you believe it? Bunch of old men, we are." He laughed.

I smiled back at him, but it wasn't a proper smile. Because no matter what had happened to me, I'd been gone six days, and Dad didn't even care enough to notice. I looked down at my plate of food. My stomach was writhing so much that my appetite faded. But I knew how hungry I was. I had to eat. As soon as I started, I scoffed it down. It vanished so fast I barely tasted it, and despite the queasy feeling in my gut, it was the best thing I'd ever eaten. The warmth spread down my throat, into my stomach, and out toward my arms and legs.

"Wow!" Dad said. "They don't feed you at that school or something? Haven't seen someone eat like that since your mum was pregnant. Back when you were nothing more than a little bean inside her. She wasn't just eating for her, she was . . ."

He trailed off, eyes watering. "She was eating for you as well."

I dropped my fork. Dad wasn't supposed to cry. I didn't know what to do. I didn't know what to say. "Dad, it's okay." The words sounded hollow, pointless. "It's all right," I said again, because saying it once just didn't feel good enough.

"Listen, this Artistic Healing stuff. I think it could work. They're good, there. When I write, everything softens. The world disappears. Does that make sense? I need you to know, I'll get better. This story—I think it could be a good one."

I took my plate to the sink, and as I turned back something caught my eye. A flash of white on the dark counter, beside the brown bag and the plastic tubs.

Sometimes when your eyes latched onto a piece of writing, like a newspaper article or a game review or a magazine headline, a word jumped up at you. Even if you didn't look at it for very long.

I glanced up to make sure Dad wasn't looking, then moved closer to the counter.

### Stormwalker
CHAPTER ONE

Jack ran toward camp, and the Darkness chased him . . .

"I knew it," I whispered.

Jack. The Darkness. I scanned the page, my breath frozen in my throat.

"I'll take those," Dad said, snatching the pages away. "I don't want you to see it yet. I'll show you when I'm a bit further in, eh?"

"It sounds scary," I said, remembering the storm again, the feeling it gave me when it got close. "I didn't know you wrote horror."

"Oh, every story has a bit of horror in it," Dad said. "But it's more than that. It's a mystery too. There's this man called the Marshal, and he's—"

"He's what?" I said, suddenly curious.

Dad tapped his nose. "I don't want to give it away," he said. "You'll have to read it. Won't be long before I'm finished, at this rate. I'm enjoying it. I've always wanted to write a story where not everything is as it seems."

Then he turned around and left me standing alone in the kitchen.

I *knew* I was right. All those links were so clear now. Cambridge. The storm. The lemon balm. It was impossible. It didn't make sense. But I was right. I knew I was.

Dad's words rang again in my mind. *The hero's a lot like you . . .*

It wasn't a dream. I wasn't imagining it or making it up. I hadn't teleported to the future. Dad wrote about a boy called Jack living in a world plagued by Darkness. And somehow—

Somehow, I was getting sucked into the pages.

I knew it sounded crazy, but it had to be true. All those days of my life, just snipped away. The back of my neck tingled at the thought of that. Because if I was right . . . if I wasn't just dreaming and Dad was transporting me into his book, then—

Then what would happen if he wrote again?

# 18

After a few minutes of standing in the silence, I headed upstairs. I checked my reflection in the mirror, just to be sure. I felt my cheeks, brushed my hair, leaned right up to the glass, blinking.

I was me. I was definitely me.

I stood there for ages, trying to get the story out of my head, the sound of Mum's voice when the Darkness closed in. It was so loud, so close.

But something about the memories of her felt ... different.

I tried to picture her, forced myself to remember her face, but it was blurry around the edges. And the blurrier it got, the more the other mum snuck in. The ill mum. The mum I didn't want to remember.

That was when I decided to do something I hadn't done since before the Longest Day.

I crept out onto the landing, listening for any noise from downstairs.

If Dad caught me doing this, he'd kill me. I hadn't heard him come up, so he must have been in the study or sitting in the living room.

Nothing. It was so quiet the only sound I could hear was the blood rushing in my ears.

*I can't believe I'm going to do this*, I thought, rubbing my clammy hands on my trousers.

I tiptoed across to Dad's bedroom door. It was open, just a crack. Just enough to see the mess inside. Clothes all over the floor, magazines and books littering the carpet. As I snuck further into the room, my eyes drifted to the photo on the bedside cabinet. It was facedown, but I knew what it was. Mum and Dad and me, smiling together at the beach.

I wanted to go over and take a proper look. That would get rid of the blurriness. But there was something else, something better, and if I didn't hurry up, I might chicken out.

I took a deep breath and turned toward Mum's wardrobe.

Three big white doors that slid open in the middle. They hadn't been touched in three hundred and seventy-one days. I was close enough to open them . . . but just thinking about it made my arms go heavy.

I reached out and touched the handle. It was so cold. I kept thinking that the last person to touch it was Mum. I closed my eyes and pictured her looking inside, and for a second I felt close to her again.

Ever since the Longest Day, it had felt like she was fading. I mean, she was there when I closed my eyes, but every day she'd been there a little bit less.

But standing there, she was clear in my mind.

Taking a deep breath, I opened the wardrobe.

Perfume. That was the first thing I noticed. Tears stung my eyes. I hadn't expected that. I didn't know why. She'd been gone for a year, but it smelled like she was in the room.

I rubbed my eyes, but the tears came back. *I shouldn't have to do this*, I thought. *She's supposed to be here. She's supposed to be here for years yet. No one else at school has got a dead mum. Some people's parents are divorced, but at least they still get to see both of them.*

I shook my head, trying to clear my thoughts.

I needed to be quick. I had to get it over and done with.

I could see what I was looking for already. It was in the box at the bottom, beside the shoes. How could one person have so many shoes? I had three pairs: one for school, one set of trainers, and one set of football cleats. Mum probably had about a million shoes in here, all different colors and shapes.

I took the box and slid the lid off. There were photos inside. Photos of Mum and Dad together, looking so young. Dad had longer hair. There were no wrinkles on his face, no bags under his eyes. And he was smiling. A proper smile that stretched all the way across his face.

Some of them had me in them. Me as a baby, me as a toddler, me on my first day at school, wearing that stupid purple sweater.

But I wasn't here for the photos. I was here for the DVD. There was a label on it that read our wedding day in big black letters. I took the case, then set the box back beside the shoes and closed the wardrobe.

I rushed out of the room and shut the door. I fell back against it, taking deep breaths. It was exactly how she left it. Those clothes were hanging like that because it was how she wanted them. Those shoes were in that order because it was how she liked it.

My heart pounded. I felt like I was going to throw up every bit of Dad's food. My eyes burned again, and I closed them tight, trying not to cry. Sometimes if you felt like you were about to cry and you didn't want to, you could think of simple things and it went away. Like a rabbit in a field or the sunrise or snow in the park. They were so easy to think about that you could concentrate on them, and the burning feeling would go away. So that was what I did now.

I headed into my room and played the DVD. I knew I shouldn't be doing it, but I had to hear her voice—her proper voice, not the one whispered to me by a freak storm.

The video started off showing all the guests arriving at the church in dresses and smart suits with flowers pinned to their chest. Dad was there before Mum. His eyes darted around and he fidgeted every few seconds.

"How are you feeling?" the cameraman asked.

"Excited. A bit sick," Dad said.

There was a cut, and a car pulled up with white ribbons draped over the hood and flags trailing from the back. Granddad stepped out and opened the passenger door.

And there was Mum, with Auntie Jane and Auntie Grace, huge smiles on their faces and flowers in their hair.

This was it. The moment I'd been waiting for. Granddad took Mum's arm and led her up the steps toward the camera, and there was that same question, "How are you feeling?"

Her eyes shone. A strand of hair fell into her face and she brushed it away. I leaned closer to the TV. I hardly dared to breathe.

"It's a dream come true," she said. Granddad squeezed her, and she rested against him, beaming. "I couldn't be happier. I'm . . . oh, you're going to make me cry!"

She swiped at her eyes, laughing. Auntie Grace inspected her, checking her makeup, and then they walked away from the camera toward the church door.

I paused the film on Mum's face. Her cheeks were rounder than I remembered. Her hair was brown and golden, like the sun shone right out of it. I left it frozen like that, just staring at her, because that was how I had to remember her. That was how I had to keep her in my mind.

Not white faced and dark eyed. Not slow and thin and drowsy. Here, her face wasn't gaunt and her eyes weren't lifeless.

There was a spark in her.

There was happiness and love and life.

I left it there for what felt like an hour, then turned off the TV. An afterimage flashed up when I blinked. Then it faded and disappeared.

When my alarm blared the next morning, I rolled out of bed, rubbing the sleep from my eyes. I stepped out onto the landing and was just about to go downstairs to make Dad's breakfast when something made me stop.

Normally his door was closed and the room was dark and full of shadows. Now it was wide open and morning light flooded through the windows.

"Dad?" I said. I headed downstairs, and opened the kitchen door to the smell of fresh coffee wafting out. And there was something else too. Something sweet. Something hot and delicious.

"Thought it'd make a change having oatmeal," Dad said, glancing at me over his shoulder.

"Yeah," I said. "Yeah, it would."

I sat at the table, watching him quietly. His hair was messy and his chin was dark and stubbly but his eyes flickered with life.

The garbage was full of takeout containers. I tied the bag up in a knot and took it out to the big recycling bin, then gathered all the empty bottles from the side of the counter and took them out too. Dad had cooked dinner for himself last night, and this morning he was doing a proper breakfast. There was a spring in his step that hadn't been there for ages, and it was all because of the writing. It had to have been.

"That's my boy," Dad said, when I got back to the warmth of the kitchen.

He ladled some oatmeal into a bowl and set it down for me. As I muttered, "Thank you," he poured himself some coffee and sat next to me, smiling the same proper smile as yesterday.

"How did the game go?" he said, as I swirled syrup into the steaming oats.

"Hmm?"

"The big match, against Westfield. I don't think I ever asked you about it."

"Oh! Um, we lost," I said, remembering the text from Danny and feeling a fresh wave of guilt. The team had needed me, and I hadn't been there.

Dad slurped his coffee and locked onto me with his tired gray eyes. "Well, you'll have a second game, right?"

"Yeah," I said. I hadn't thought of that. I crossed my fingers under the counter, praying I didn't miss that game too. I didn't think Danny would ever forgive me if I did.

"Was thinking I might be able to pop down. You know, cheer you on. Help you send them packing."

"Really?" I stared at his face, trying to see if he meant it. Even just talking about going out was a big improvement. "That'd be really good."

Dad sipped his coffee and turned back to the window. Was he sitting up straighter? His shoulders weren't slumping like they normally did. He turned back to me. There was a spark in his eyes, a flash of his old self. All the pieces that had broken apart when Mum died—the things that made him *him*—just for a moment it was like they'd joined back together again.

And that was when I realized . . .

The only thing that had changed was the writing.

Maybe I jumped into Dad's story for a reason. Maybe—

Maybe if I finished it, I'd get my dad back. Properly back, I mean. He'd be like this all the time and the bags under his eyes would disappear and he'd come to watch me play football again.

All I had to do now was figure out *how*.

# 19

Danny avoided me at school that day.

I tried sitting next to him for roll call, but he just moved away. Every time I went to approach him about the match, he saw me coming and walked in the other direction.

"Give it a few hours," Slogger said, when we lined up outside Math. "He'll come round."

But he didn't come round for the rest of the day, and he didn't come round on the bus on the way home, either. By the time I got there, he was sitting in our usual place at the back, but none of the other seats were free. I sat on my own at the front, trying to take my mind off it.

Why wouldn't he just talk to me? I needed him to know I couldn't help it. I never asked to jump into Dad's story. I didn't have any control over it. He wrote, and somehow

I got dragged into it. It happened so fast . . . and, I knew, thinking about it, it would happen again. It was just a matter of time.

As soon as the bus stopped, I ran off and walked quickly home. Danny would just ignore me again anyway, and I didn't want to argue with him.

That thought kept flowing through my head: *It will happen again.*

And it did. It happened again that night.

I was running down the wing on FIFA, about to cross the ball in when I felt the tug in my gut. I fluffed the kick and looked down as my stomach wrenched and a million butterflies exploded in every direction.

Then I looked up, and a shiver ran through me.

My bedroom was gone. Everything was gone. I was back under the dome, in the stark light of the market square. I scrambled to my feet, breathing quickly. I was back. The storm was raging above the camp, just like last time.

*Am I in Dad's mind right now?* I thought. *Or is it another world, some strange new reality that he's created just by writing?* I didn't know how it worked, I only knew that it did. I was back—back in the story—and I had to figure out how to finish it.

"Jack?" Iris said. She was leading me toward the edge of camp, with kids rushing past us and robots grinding in the rubble-strewn alleys.

"Sorry," I said. "What are we doing?"

She eyed me warily. "Farming."

I looked toward the distant fields, if you could call them fields when there was no grass on them. People were already working there, digging on their hands and knees. "How long's it been since the Stormwalking? Have I . . . have I missed any time here?" If I missed time back in real life, maybe it would be the same here.

"We only went out yesterday. Why would you miss time? What do you mean?"

"It's hard to explain," I said. I shivered, remembering the storm getting so close last time, remembering the cold and the sound of Mum's voice. "Are we going out again tonight?"

"We go out every night," she said, then laughed, seeing the look on my face. "It's not always that bad. Usually we get two or three runs in—enough for the generators, and to power the radio tower on the hill."

I thought back to my first night here, and the Darkness peeling away from the headlights.

"Can't you just—you know—drive out there in a pocket of daylight?"

"There are some areas the truck can't get to," Iris said. "Especially when the road breaks down. The Darkness changes the landscape every night. Anyway, I told you, glowroot only grows in Darkness. As soon as the light touches it, it dies."

"So they send us out into the storm. A bunch of kids."

"We're dupes," Iris said, shrugging. "Get used to it."

We passed the remains of an old fence. It had been ripped out and chopped up until only stubs remained, buried in the dry soil.

"If anyone hears you asking this many questions, they'll report you. I thought you said you could—you know—look into Jack's mind, or something."

"I can. Or, at least, I thought I could. But lately he's been distant. Ever since—"

"Ever since what?"

"Since I saw the memories of his dad. Since I saw him getting dragged away. Like all the children here—taken because we were duplicates."

Iris was quiet for a moment. The only sound was the *crunch-crunch-crunch* of the dry ground beneath our feet as we walked onward again.

"I volunteered, actually," she said quietly.

*What?*

I stopped in my tracks. Jack's dad hid him under the stairs to avoid him becoming a Stormwalker, but Iris—she wasn't just given up, she *wanted* to be one . . .

"Why would you do that?" I asked, searching her eyes.

"I had my reasons," she said.

I stared at her, desperate to know more, but I'd seen that look before and I knew better than to press her, so I changed the subject.

"It must have been bad, back in the City. I mean, a Duplication Act? I thought this was supposed to be the future."

"They were out of options. Mrs. Cloud said they had to tax floor space, and even that didn't work. The City was big, but not big enough for so many people. So the Marshals sent us out to find somewhere we could live, and grow food without the storm killing everything. It's not *that* bad," she said. "When we get through to the City, they'll be able to expand. Some people can live here, and some can live in the City. There'll be room to spread out. The Act will be lifted."

Her words hung in the air. I didn't know what to say, so I walked in silence, letting it sink in. We were approaching the dried-up field where our group was Farming. A river ran alongside it—the River Cam, I guessed. Back home there would have been ducks swimming in it and moorhens panicking if you got too close. Here there was just the steady whisper of the water.

Beside the river, the earth was scorched and blackened. A dozen people were digging up the ground, some with shovels, some with just their bare hands.

At the edge of the field, I noticed someone running sprints back and forth along the tree line.

Seth. The guy who organized the Stormwalking last time I was here. He must have been on a different timetable from us.

"He's the Pathfinder," Iris said, as if that explained everything. "He doesn't have to Farm. He has to chart the glowroot, to help us grab as much of it as possible."

She handed me a shovel from a heavy-lidded container, and I followed her toward an empty patch of dirt. In the distance, I could make out what looked like corn growing. But we were planting potatoes and millet, the sort of thing that could grow in harsh weather, I guessed.

I wasn't as fast as Iris, but it felt good to be doing something.

Ever since the storm hit, everything had been a jumbled rush, but this—

When I dug the shovel into the earth, it scraped and crunched just like when Dad did the gardening at home. It felt real. It was tiring work. Even though it wasn't particularly hot in the faint gray light, my rags grew sticky with sweat.

What kind of government would send kids into a storm that wiped out the world? They must have been very desperate, or very disturbed, or both.

I thought about Dad, back home in his study, making all this up. Where did it come from? I'd always seen him as being quite happy, up until this year anyway, but this . . . this didn't come from the mind of a happy man. Thinking that made me want to finish the story more than ever.

Bracing myself, I tried to access Jack's memories again. I didn't want to push it, and I *definitely* didn't want to feel as sick as it made me last time, but if I was going to finish the story I had to be able to get inside Jack's head.

It had been so vivid before. Those memories of his dad . . . he'd been taken on Icarus 1, but where were they going? Maybe I had to find out if he was still alive. Maybe I could track him down, somehow. Unite our camp with theirs.

But that didn't solve the mystery. What was it Dad said? *I've always wanted to write a story where not everything is as it seems.* There was some kind of puzzle to figure out, and I was at the heart of it—I had to be. That was why I kept jumping here.

"Have you ever heard from the other Icarus projects?" I asked.

Iris shook her head. "We've been trying to reach them for months. If LRP got through, we'd know about it," she said.

"Why only months?"

"What do you mean?"

"LRP haven't been trying to trace them for longer?"

"Jack," she said, frowning at me, "we've only been here six months. It takes time."

I dropped the shovel with a clatter. It had taken a while for the thoughts to slot into place, but now that they had, I couldn't shake them. *We've only been here six months*, she said, but I'd seen Jack's thoughts, and I knew that wasn't true. We were taken when we were eight years old, and yeah, they trained us at the City before we left, but not for three years.

"Are you all right?" she said, passing the shovel back to me.

"Yeah," I lied. Six months? It would be impossible to build such a big camp in six months. Couldn't she see that? It would take ages to set the perimeter, to carve out a hall in the cellars under the university. To get their systems in place, running like clockwork.

Just then something moved above us. The Darkness was fading at the top of the dome. Its writhing tendrils flickered as it slithered away. The clouds above us now were gray, not black. They didn't seethe and ripple with life. They didn't screech or howl.

The Darkness retreated until it was no more than a distant shadow on the horizon. Then when I blinked again, the storm was gone. With a sound like a great, electronic moan, the floodlights cut off.

What was going on? Ever since I'd been here, the storm had been an ever-present threat. It was always there. Then I thought back to the first jump. We were out of camp, weren't we? We were trying to escape it as the clouds shot closer. Out in a pocket of daylight. This must have been another one. But time was different here, wasn't it?

The constant yellow glow had been replaced with real, natural light. It wasn't daylight, not exactly. The sky above us was clouded over, a blanket of gray, like evening wanted to approach but didn't know how to go about it. It felt better than the floodlights. But how long would it last?

I rubbed my arms to get rid of the goose bumps. Before, I could only see as far as the protective barrier allowed, but now—

Now I could see how far the wasteland stretched.

"The whole town's like this," I whispered. The words sounded hollow.

"The whole *world's* like this," Iris said.

I turned toward her. The disbelief must have shown on my face, because she laughed, and said, "You really were telling the truth, weren't you? About not being from around here?"

"What made you change your mind?"

"No one could fake a look like that." She scrutinized me for so long that it made me turn away. "I don't understand it. It doesn't make any sense whatsoever. But I don't think you're lying."

"Thanks," I said. I tried to imagine what it might feel like if Danny suddenly changed, if he told *me* he had someone else inside him, someone from years and years in the past.

"What's your name then?" she whispered, making sure there was no one close enough to hear. "Your real name? You *do* have a name?"

"Of course I do. I'm Owen. Owen Smith."

"Owen," she said slowly, testing the word. "It doesn't suit you. You don't mind if I keep calling you Jack, do you? It feels right, that way. Plus—" she glanced around to check no one was listening—"it's probably for the best. I'm not sure anyone else will believe that you're a pre-Dark trapped inside Jack's body."

"No," I said, struggling to suppress a laugh. "I think I can forgive you."

She looked toward the horizon. "Come on. Lights down means we've got Hunting to do. And then . . ."

"Then what?" I said, when she didn't offer any more.

"Then we'll get you some bottle caps. You owe me, remember?"

# 20

We met with the other Stormwalkers at the edge of camp. They weren't all following our timetable—some of them had come from other classes—but I guessed that the pocket of daylight meant they had to drop what they were doing and make the most of it.

"How long does it last?" I whispered to Iris, indicating the gray sky.

"It's different every time. Could be minutes, could be hours. Be ready."

I didn't need to ask her what for. The memory of that first jump still haunted me, the way the Darkness made me feel when it got so close. All those memories of Mum.

Dillon nodded at me like Danny did when he spotted me across the courtyard at school. There was a large group of us here, all kids around my age, all in the same grubby rags.

"It's a good day for Hunting," he said, eyeing us as we got closer. "I hope you're ready. One hour, max. I don't want anyone to get caught out."

He looked at me as he said it, and my cheeks burned. Something told me he was referring to my trip to Cleansing on that first night. I tried to hold his gaze because it wasn't like I could have helped it. I just woke up here—I didn't know what was going on.

When he started talking again, my eyes drifted past him to the distant road and buildings. We were actually going out there. Into the wasteland. I held my breath, wondering how far we would be expected to go. When Quinn picked us up in his truck, we were quite a ways out . . .

I didn't fancy another mad sprint if the Darkness reemerged earlier than expected. Especially without our illuminators.

"Carter and Dillon, you take the north side," Seth said. "Jack, Iris, I'd like you to take the hill to the south. Yvonne, we can go this way. Remember, keep an eye out for gasoline. You've got a hose in your pack if you need to use it." He handed each of us a small bag attached to a belt. "Stay sharp. Stay safe."

And with that, he ran off, dust trailing behind him and pebbles pinging up with every step.

Iris grinned at me, then dashed toward the hill. I blinked in surprise, and my heart kicked up a gear. I felt as if I'd got a bad start in a race.

"Hold up!" I called after her, my feet scuffing on the crumbled earth until we reached the road, where it evened out underfoot.

"You've got to stay on your toes," Iris said. "There could be Dreamless out here."

I thought back to that creature we saw when we went Stormwalking: its pasty skin, the wild, frothing mouth. "Iris—what, er, what *are* the Dreamless?"

She hesitated, her jaw set, and her expression made me grow cold.

"I don't know what they are. I only know what they were. Family. Friends. People who got exposed to the Darkness for too long and had everything ripped out of their minds. Don't worry about them. If you see one, just whistle. I'll be right behind you."

"Whistle?"

"Yeah, like this," she said, putting her little fingers to the corners of her mouth and blasting out a long note. "If I hear that, I'll always find you."

"Thanks," I said, although I wasn't sure how much better it made me feel.

I'd been along this road loads of times in my world. There was a supermarket and a brilliant cake shop. Not here though, even though some of the buildings were mostly intact. Small holes in the walls and broken windows were the only signs of the Darkness getting too close. But farther along the road they quickly lost their shape, until it was impossible to tell they ever were buildings.

We picked up the pace, jogging to the top of the hill. Bricks and rubble were strewn across the road.

"Keep an eye out for anything that looks useful," Iris called. She slowed down just enough for me to catch up, scanning the edges of the road.

"How do you know what's useful?"

"You just know," Iris said. She crouched down, picking through stones and dust, moving aside bricks. "You know when you see it. Like that," she said, her gaze latching onto a broken shopfront.

Something glistened in the light. She rushed over and bent to scoop it up.

It was an empty beer bottle, just like the ones Dad left lying round the house.

"What's so special about that?" I took it off her and held it up to the light. You could see where the label used to be, so faded it was impossible to read. "It's just a bottle."

"You never know when glass might come in handy," she said, snatching it back and placing it carefully in her bag. "And anyway, I like this stuff."

Did I imagine it, or were her cheeks going red?

"The others just go for the obvious things. Soap, weapons, that kind of thing. They don't care what it is. I . . . like the boring, everyday stuff. I like to know how people lived."

Iris had half-filled her bag before I picked up a single object. She grabbed key rings, an old pocket watch, even something that looked like a plastic toy. Who knew that could survive an apocalypse?

"Oh, wow," she said, clambering through a crumbled doorway.

I followed her in, covering my nose against the stale air. She kicked aside a clump of stone, and picked something up. Dust fell away beneath her fingers.

"What is it?" I asked, moving closer. She held it so carefully I thought it really *was* precious, but as I got closer I saw—

"It's just a book."

"Just a book?" she squealed, recoiling. She blew on the cover, sending dust billowing into the air. "This is an antique. *Urban fantasy,*" she read, squinting at the blurb on the back. She opened it and whispered, "Look, it was published in 2001." Then she laughed, like it was the best possible thing she could find, and stuffed it in her bag.

I was just about to dig through the rubble when a sudden noise made me stop.

I held my breath, listening.

Iris's eyes locked onto mine, and I knew she'd heard it too—a clatter, somewhere in the ruin. I strained my ears, but there was only silence, heavy all around us.

"We should leave," Iris whispered.

I nodded, backing away slowly.

We were the only ones who'd come up this way. It couldn't have been another Stormwalker. And if the noise wasn't us, then—

A flash of movement in the shadows.

Bricks crunched and pinged as something lurched out of the gloom.

I tried to cry out, but the dust clogged my throat and all that came out was a strangled yelp. Iris rushed past me and I turned to follow her, but as I did something gripped my ankle and threw me over. I threw my hands up to stop myself smashing into the rough ground.

"Iris!"

The rubble dug into my elbows, cutting my skin as I was dragged back. Panic swelling inside me, I tried to grab hold of something, anything, but the ground offered nothing.

I spun around and lashed out with my leg, kicking as hard as I could—

And that was when I saw it.

Dark patches swelled under its shallow white eyes and purple blotches bloomed on its pasty skin. Its nails were long and yellow, sharpened to points, and its teeth . . .

Its teeth gnashed and ground, as rivulets of drool dribbled down its chin.

"Get off!" I cried, swallowing back the lump in my throat.

I kicked again and connected with its feral face, but it only snarled, eyes flashing, and leapt at me once more. Desperately I scrabbled back, trying to get away—

*Thwack.*

A heavy stone smashed into its forehead, and scattered across the ground.

A groan slipped out of the creature's foaming mouth, then it collapsed, unconscious.

"Th-thank you," I panted, scrambling to my feet and fighting for breath.

Iris didn't move, staring at the creature's lifeless body. She had a slingshot in her hands, another stone already loaded. Now that the Dreamless had stopped moving, it looked so . . . skinny. How could it have been that fast? That strong? I rubbed my ankle where those long, pale fingers had gripped me so ferociously.

"There could be more," Iris said. "We should get back and warn LRP."

# 21

The Dreamless flashed in my mind every time I blinked. Lurching white hands, blank eyes, and withered skin. Was that what happened when you touched the Darkness? It turned you into that?

*Calm down, Owen. You're safe.*

Or as safe as I could be, anyway, when I was trapped inside a disaster story.

We scrambled back, Iris with her pack full of objects, me with far less. We passed a robot, but it barely had time to say, "Hello . . . STORMWALKERS," before we were past it and pelting toward the market square.

It was deserted. Iris grabbed my arm and dragged me on.

"This way," she said.

There was a small building near the edge of camp, almost a hut, but not quite, the sort of thing you see next to train stations in quiet villages.

Iris sprinted toward it, bursting through the door.

Quinn was hunched over a desk. All across the wall behind it were screens and dials—dozens of dials. He looked up, frowning. There were two other people in there too. I recognized the man I saw as we burst into camp on my first trip here. The third person was a woman; an LRP officer I'd never seen before.

"You two are back early," Quinn said.

"Dreamless," Iris panted, "over by Regent Street."

"Was it them?" he said, jumping to his feet. Iris shook her head. "Okay, good. Stay here and grab something to eat. We'll take care of it . . ."

I shot Iris a look, wondering what Quinn had meant. "Was it *who*?"

All the color drained from her cheeks. In the pallid glow of the lights she looked like a ghost. Quinn nodded at the woman, who set off in the direction we'd just come from. He stood up and started rummaging through a cabinet beside the table.

The quiet stretched for so long I thought Iris was going to ignore the question, but then she spoke in this tiny, low voice, and it was all I could do just to hear the words.

"My parents," she said. "They got caught by the storm back in the City. It got them just as they reached the barrier. They tried to Cleanse them, but . . ."

"I'm sorry," I said.

The words sounded so pathetic, lingering there between us.

"I've seen Dad once since we got here. What used to be Dad, anyway. I don't know how he got so far from the

City without a ship, but Quinn said Dreamless can walk for days in search of . . ."

I knew what she couldn't say. It was there in Jack's thoughts, bubbling to the surface. In search of *people.* They were drawn to us, drawn to what they used to be, before the endless fear warped their minds and bodies.

No wonder she was so determined for me to go back to Cleansing when I first jumped here. I didn't know about the camp or the City or Stormwalking or the Dreamless. I didn't know *anything*, and she thought the Cleansing hadn't worked. She thought the storm was going to turn me into one of those things.

"That's why I volunteered," Iris said. "My brother went to live with my aunt and uncle, but they couldn't afford the space for me. And anyway, you heard the ads. Do well here, and your family will get rewarded."

I stared at her. I didn't know what to say. She turned away, gazing at the radio—

There was a crackle of static, then a voice came through.

"This is Icarus 1, do you read?"

The fog in my head evaporated on the spot. Jack's thoughts screamed to the front of my mind. My heart leapt into my throat, trying to beat its way out of my body.

"This is Icarus 1, do you copy? Is anybody out there? The City is dead. Repeat, the City is dead. We need to initiate Operation Phoenix."

Every bit of air squeezed out of my lungs. That voice . . . I knew it from somewhere. But what did he mean about the City being dead? Surely if it was, we'd know about it by now. Wouldn't we? Jack's brother, Ayden, was there. I could see his face as clear as if it were my own. I saw all of them, the crowd of people back behind the fence, waving as our airship set off, drifting higher and higher into the air. We were supposed to save them. They couldn't be dead . . .

Iris was standing there, her mouth hanging open.

James was the first to react. He slammed a button on the dashboard. "We read you, Icarus 1," he said. "Icarus 3, reading you loud and clear."

Silence.

Iris's eyes were wide. My own face was frozen. If the City was dead, what did that mean for us? Were we the last survivors? Just us, and the other Icarus projects?

Quinn turned to Iris, then back to me, as if seeing us clearly for the first time. I couldn't read the expression on his face.

"It's good to hear your voice, Icarus 3. What are your coordinates? We've got a pre-Dark airbase here—we think we might be able to reach you."

"One one one, three two—"

Quinn slammed his fist on a button, and the line went dead.

James gaped at him.

What had just happened? I thought the whole point of setting up this camp was to find somewhere to live, and then to tell people about it. The Marshal said they'd never had any word from Icarus 1 or 2, so this was the first contact they'd ever made, and Quinn just cut them off?

"Quinn!" Iris said.

"What are you doing? Quinn, that was—"

"I *know* what it was," Quinn said, holding up his hands defensively. "But we need to tell the Marshal about it. It could be a trap. We don't know the City's dead—for all we know, Icarus 1 might be compromised."

"Don't be ridiculous," James said pleadingly, "my . . . my family—Quinn, if they're dead . . ."

"We don't know that they are," Quinn said gently. "Our first priority has to be the safety of this camp. We need to keep this quiet, at least for now. If the City *is* dead, the Marshal will know what to do. We can reestablish contact after we've spoken to him. If word got out . . ."

James sat down, breathing heavily. He held his head in his hands.

"You're right. Of course you are. The Marshal . . . yes . . ."

"James—help Sarah deal with the Dreamless," Quinn said, before turning to face us. There was a look in his eyes that I couldn't figure out. "I'll take care of this."

I couldn't get control of Jack's thoughts. It felt like icicles were stabbing my mind, all the images swirling and swirling.

Then it hit me. What was so familiar about that voice.

The man on the radio . . . he was Jack's dad.

He was alive. After everything! They'd taken him away from the City, shoved him on board with the other Stormwalkers on Icarus 1, and now he'd managed to find us. He was *alive*! This was it. This was what I had to do. I had to get through to him. I had to let him know I was okay.

"Come on," Quinn said. "We better go."

He led us to the church, the only building on the market square that remained mostly intact. My stomach churned with every step. I breathed slowly, trying to calm down. I could feel my legs moving, but it was as if they were controlled by someone else.

Jack's dad was alive!

But . . . if the City really was dead, then what did that mean for the rest of Jack's family? For *all* their families? We were supposed to be here to save the City. To build them a new home and let them know about it, so they could send people here to live—to survive. Had it all been for nothing?

We stopped outside the church. The oak double doors had been eaten away and replaced with moth-eaten curtains, which hung either side of the arch. Quinn waited for a few Stormwalkers to pass, taking their scavenged items to the stalls on the square, then he bent low, his expression grave.

"Listen to me very carefully," he said. "I know you'll have questions about what you just heard. Trust me, I do too. But for your own safety, you have to ignore it. Just for now. Promise me you won't mention it. You won't go round asking questions. If the Marshal finds out what you just heard, then . . ."

"Quinn . . . ," Iris said.

"Trust me. I'll find you soon, and explain it all then. But for now, just . . . just get back to the timetable. You've still got time before the daylight pocket closes. Don't mention this to anybody."

He turned to me, as if he wanted to say more, but the words had got stuck. Eyes watering, he whirled on the spot and marched through the curtains.

My heart was beating loud and hard. I didn't know if the City really was dead, but I did know one thing. Jack's dad wasn't a liar.

I turned to Iris. Her face was ashen. Of course . . . if that message was true, then she'd lost her aunt and uncle, and her brother too. So many lives lost . . .

"You remember when you asked about the Chamber?" she said.

"Yeah?"

"It's below this building. This is where they take the people who break the rules." She crept up to the curtains, pressing her ear up against them. "Are you thinking what I'm thinking?"

But before I could reply, she snuck inside.

"Iris—wait!"

Hesitating just for a second, to make sure no one was watching, I followed her. There were no pews inside the church. Just an empty space with boarded-up windows, a muddy flagstone floor, and the gray sky instead of a roof.

Up ahead, where the altar should have been, there was a desk and a high-backed chair. The Marshal was sitting in it, listening to someone whispering in his ear.

His face . . . he didn't look anything like the cheering, inspiring man who had encouraged everyone in the hall the other night. His sunken eyes looked too small for his head, and his skin was chalky and stretched too thin. He looked tired—and something else . . . He looked mad.

"What is it?" he said, waving the first man away as Quinn approached.

"There's been contact on the radio."

"*What?*" The Marshal's nostrils flared. "The radio tower's supposed to be broken."

"It is. The main one, for communicating with the City. None of the guys on my team will ever be able to get through, just like you wanted. But the short-range beacons have always been active. The contact came from Icarus 1."

"What did they say?" the Marshal demanded.

"That the City is dead. Only James heard it," Quinn said quickly. "I managed to convince him it would be dangerous to talk to them without your permission."

"Good," the Marshal said. "Very good. Has he been to Cleansing yet this week?"

"I don't think so . . ."

"He can go today. Oversee the questioning. Make sure he knows we've only been here six months. The City is alive and well. There's been no contact from the other Icarus projects, but we're holding out hope. You know the drill."

Quinn turned, and I ducked down low, holding my breath. I didn't dare look up. I strained my ears, listening for any footsteps on the flagstone floor. But none came. He must have still been over by the Marshal's desk. Had he seen me? I glanced at Iris beside me. Her eyes were wide. If we got discovered . . . best not to think about that.

"What is it?" said the Marshal. "What are you waiting for?"

"It was Ryan," Quinn said.

"What?"

"On the radio. It was Ryan. You told me he died with the others, back in the City. I've been looking after Jack, thinking his dad was dead, but all this time he's been alive."

I couldn't hide anymore. I had to look up. I had to see.

Quinn was standing over the desk, towering over the Marshal. Even from here I could see he was shaking. Jack's thoughts were going crazy. I tried to hold them at bay, so I could listen properly. I wanted to move closer, but I didn't dare.

"He hid that boy from us," the Marshal said. "He hid a duplicate."

"So did thousands of others. Did you send them on a ship too?"

"He was a Marshal—"

"This is about the vote of no confidence, isn't it? He was going to get you deposed as head of the council. You were going to be exiled, and you didn't want any of it. You were hoping he'd die, weren't you? Well how's that plan looking now? He's alive! We could unite with them. It's what we have to do. What's stopping me from getting him back on the line?"

"The boy," the Marshal said coldly. The silence that followed was the loudest I'd ever heard. "If you make one move—*one move*—the boy gets it. Do you understand?"

# 22

The Marshal's words rang in my ears after we snuck back out into the quiet square. He'd acted as if hearing from Icarus 1 wasn't big news, but it was massive, surely? They'd been waiting for word ever since they established camp.

*If you make one move, the boy gets it . . .*

For some reason, he was using me to manipulate Quinn. I thought the whole point of the Icarus projects was to find a new home for the people of the City, but if those people were dead, shouldn't everyone know about it?

"I didn't know that was your dad on the radio," Iris said, looking at me with obvious concern. "Are you all right? That can't have been very nice to hear."

"We've got to stop him," I said. "We've got to stop the Marshal." I couldn't piece it together yet, but something wasn't right. About the whole camp. About everything. "There must be a way to get through to Icarus 1."

"The radio tower." Iris's eyes widened. The emptiness that had filled them when we heard the message about the City? It had disappeared—at least for the time being. "The Marshal said it was broken. Well, if we go over there when we Stormwalk tonight, maybe we can figure out a way to fix it."

We used the last of the daylight pocket to scavenge some Band-Aids, a few pieces of scrap metal, and another tank of gasoline from the back half of a broken motorbike. We traded the metal for four caps, which bought us a potato cake each and a bowl of seeds for dessert.

The Stormwalking was announced after we finished eating, and the camp filed into the hall as one big group. I stood next to Iris and Dillon at the back of the room, beside the generator.

A hush descended as the Marshal walked in. Was I imagining it, or did he look straight at me? He started talking about the day's Hunting haul and the importance of attending lessons to "safeguard our country's history." I choked down a laugh when he said that. I mean, they weren't exactly safeguarding it, were they? They thought a Slinky was a weapon.

"We are the City's only hope," he said, and this time he definitely looked right at me. But the City was dead. I believed that one hundred percent. Otherwise, why wouldn't Quinn question it? What I didn't get was why the Marshal was so keen to cover it up. "Our families are out there, desperate to find us. Restock our glowroot, and we *will* make contact. We will reunite with them. We will save them."

Seth split us up into teams again, and handed out the gear. As I threw mine on, I walked over to him, trying to act casually in case the Marshal was watching. Ever since that incident with Quinn, he was really creeping me out.

"Send me to the tower," I said. "Please."

"Me too," Iris said, appearing beside me.

"What?" Seth's eyebrows shooting up in surprise. "Why?"

"Just—," I began, but Iris interrupted me.

"There's something I want to check," she said. "I was reading about it in *Ten Secrets of the Pre-Dark World*."

"We'll bring back more glowroot than you can shake a corn round at," I added, smiling.

Seth snorted. "I was going to send you to the foot of the barren caves, but I can send Eddie, Sian, and Tyler there instead. You'll need a third, though. You know you can't go out in pairs."

"I'll go with them," said Dillon. He shrugged when I looked at him. "May as well—it's as good a place as any."

I wondered who he had left at the City. Would he be so eager to run out into the Darkness if he knew it was all for nothing? Of course not. None of them would. No wonder the Marshal was so keen to keep it a secret.

As we jogged toward the tunnel, our illuminators glowing brighter in the shadows, the Marshal boomed: "I will leave you now with this thought. The pre-Darks believed in legendary lights, called *stars*. In the histories, they are described as shrines, high in the sky, where the greatest heroes lived on after death, shining for eternity. You may well be duplicates, but you are far from unnecessary. Help bring proof of our safe camp back to the City, and you will take your place among the greatest heroes to ever walk this earth."

The radio tower stood on top of a lump of jagged rock, higher than any other point around camp. Each of the Icarus projects had a communication device built into its airship. It only had two simple messages: either they'd set up a safe haven, or they hadn't.

But since Icarus 3 crashed, the device shattered, and they'd had to build their own way of getting through to the City. It worked through glowroot, just like all the other technology in camp, and was powerful enough to reach through the Darkness.

That was the theory, anyway.

I was looking forward to seeing what it actually looked like, after hearing the Marshal talking with Quinn. But before we could take any glowroot over there, we had to stockpile some back at camp—and that meant having a smooth run, without facing off against any Dreamless.

The Darkness was waiting for us at the broken section of the tunnel. It hissed all around us, and I could hear Mum's voice again already, as if she was right there beside me, as if she was everywhere at once.

*"I'm sorry," Mum said, and I could see her now, the tears trickling down her face—*

*"I'm so sorry, Owen."*

"It's playing on your fears," Iris called. "Don't let it in. Don't let it close."

The storm pulled at me like a giant magnet. I wrenched myself back, shaking my head to clear Mum out of it. I focused on happy thoughts, from before she told me, from before she got so weak. Painting together and walking on the beach and picnics in the park, the real park with fresh green grass and waddling ducks and circling, singing birds.

And after a while, my legs felt less heavy.

The illuminators cast only enough light to see a few feet ahead of us. Every now and then I slipped and stumbled, but we kept going, following the curve of the river, away from the distant glow of the camp.

Finally we reached a lamp, and slowed down to catch our breath.

There was a clunk and a groan above us as the motion-sensitive light flared on. The Darkness peeled back, higher and higher into the sky. The first meadow was only a hundred yards away.

"There's another lamp ahead of us," Iris said. "About twenty yards."

She grabbed a stone and loaded it in her slingshot. She took aim and fired, sending it soaring into the distance. The Darkness gobbled it up, then it scuffed the rough ground ahead of us. There was a brief hum, and a light appeared, about thirty yards away.

"It's there," she said. "You just have to trust it."

The light flickered and died. A shiver ran down my arms, making the hairs stand on end.

We were going to have to be fast . . .

Iris gave the signal and Dillon bolted after her. I ran, adrenaline coursing through me as the Darkness raged. The illuminators gave off a bright glow, but it wasn't big enough to keep the storm at bay completely, and every time the clouds got close a stabbing pain lanced through me.

We made it to a second lamp, and a third, but after that the lights ran out. Maybe it was too hard to keep them powered this far from the generator, or maybe the storm had broken them. Either way, we had to rely on our illuminators as our sole protection.

Thankfully the glowroot wasn't far away. We pulled up, panting hard. The air out here was colder than in camp, and there was a bitter taste to it. It smelled a bit like those beans Dad had burned the other day.

I followed Iris's lead, carefully plucking the flowers and storing them in the special compartment on the back of my jacket. Each piece of glowroot had its own individual container, where it would be protected from the light. These could detach from the bag, and be stored for whenever they were needed.

Seth passed us in midharvest, running off in the opposite direction with his group. We joined up with Anja and the others on our first trip back to the tunnel. Then Dillon, Iris, and I ran back, clambering over mounds of rubble, working our way to the distant tower. Using tufts of long-dead black grass, I hauled myself up, my feet skidding on loose chunks of rock. The tower was easy to see, even though the Darkness shrouded it, because the power station below it gave off an ethereal green glow.

"Let's see what we find, shall we?" Iris said.

There was another meadow just outside the glowing, block-shaped building. As we approached, the Darkness slammed down, screeching madly at us, as if it knew it wouldn't stand a chance when we got close.

I was so determined to fight off the memories of *my* parents that I must have let my guard down, because the next thing I knew, Jack's dad flew to the surface of my mind.

*"No," he said, a whimpering tone to his voice as he dug through broken bricks and splintered wood. "It can't be gone. It can't be . . ."*

*He was in the City—the remains of it, anyway—the light of his airship blasting away the Darkness in a small bubble, but even that was enough to see the destruction.*

"Come on," Dillon said, grabbing my arm. "We can't stop."

I gritted my teeth, swatting the image away. We ran together, the three of us, over to the next meadow, and as we reached it, the storm pulled back angrily.

We gathered as much glowroot as we could. Then Iris stood, and turned to face the doorway to the power station. The tower loomed over us, surrounded by swirling clouds of Darkness.

"I'm going in," she said.

"What?" Dillon spluttered. "We can't—we've got to take this back to the camp."

But Iris wasn't listening. She was already striding off, toward a shrouded door. As she approached, a light hummed on, one of those motion-sensitive ones I'd seen on the first Stormwalking, leading the way inside.

"If the Marshal finds out—"

"He won't," I said, although how I knew that, I couldn't say. I just knew I had to do something. Without waiting for Dillon, I followed Iris into the power station. It wasn't long before I heard Dillon's footsteps behind me.

"Hey!" he called. "Wait up!"

More lights hummed into life before us, until the entranceway opened up into a large room, bigger than our entire house back home. In the middle of the room was a circular metal stand, and on top of it was some kind of container—a shimmering silver lantern of glass, with an ethereal orb inside it, drifting and pulsing. At its very center, the light was pure white, but its edges glowed green and blue. It hung in a sort of mist. On each of the lantern's four corners, a metal rod shot up into the ceiling. Up to where the radio tower loomed in the storm.

"Well, the energy capsule's still on," said Iris.

I couldn't see any controls. The rest of the room was bare—just plain white walls. No TV screens, like the main hall in camp, no noticeboard, no nothing.

Iris took out her glowroot and dropped it in the hole at the top of the capsule.

There was a clink and a sudden crackle, the orb of light blossomed, its ghostly edges twining, pressing up against the glass, then it settled once more.

"Why did you want to come here?" Dillon asked. "What's wrong?"

Iris dropped some more glowroot inside the capsule. "Nothing," Iris said. "That's the problem. It's just like it's always been. I don't understand. Unless . . ."

She shot me a look, and I knew right away what she was thinking. It was just like being with Danny. *Unless it never worked in the first place.*

# 23

My mind spun.

A wave of grogginess washed over me, and I steadied myself, trying not to fall over. When the rushing settled, I opened my eyes slowly, hardly daring to look. I knew these walls. I . . . I was inside my house. My real house, back in my life.

The smell of food filled my nostrils. Dad must have been cooking dinner. I closed my eyes again, waiting for Jack's thoughts to drift away. It was so hard to think . . .

If the tower had never worked, then the whole camp had been risking their lives for nothing. What was the Marshal playing at? I knew we were duplicates, but surely he wasn't that crazy?

Dad called me from the kitchen, but his voice was buried in the clattering and banging.

When I felt sure-footed enough to stand properly, I walked toward the doorway, thinking about last time—how he couldn't remember where I'd been. I hesitated. How much time had I missed now? It was Thursday when I jumped. It must have been, because it was the day after the Westfield game.

Holding my breath, I dug inside my pocket for my phone. The date flashed up: Saturday.

Another day gone! Just completely vanished. I remembered playing FIFA on Thursday night, and then nothing—nothing except the story. The Dreamless. The radio call. The tower . . .

Surely this time Dad would have realized?

"Thought I'd get started on dinner," he said, when I opened the door. "Got something big planned. Something nice."

He winked at me and even managed a full smile again. It made his face crinkle up around the edges. He looked so much older now than he did last year. I guessed the Longest Day changed him on the outside as well as on the inside.

"Dad?" I said, the worried thoughts still bouncing around in my head. I kept thinking about the missing days. What happened to me in real life while I was inside the story? Was I still here? Did I pass out somewhere? I needed to find a way to word it, so he wouldn't get freaked out.

"Yeah?"

"I really enjoyed kicking the ball around with you yesterday."

"Kicking the ball?" he said. He looked up from the pan he was stirring on the hob and frowned.

"Yeah, after school. At the park."

I knew we wouldn't have played football at the park. We used to do it all the time, but we haven't been for ages.

"Oh ... um ... yeah. Yeah," he said slowly. "How could I have forgotten that?" He looked at me, his face creasing. "But I suppose we must have ..."

I could tell he was struggling to put it all together. He knew we didn't kick the ball around, just like I did. I wanted to text Danny, but we hadn't spoken since I missed the match. So I quickly sent a message to Slogger, without caring how odd it sounded.

Was I at school yesterday?

His reply came back in a few seconds.

What are you on about? Course you were.

Then another:

Er, now you mention it, I'm not sure. Why?

Dad couldn't remember what we did yesterday, and Slogger didn't know I if I was at school or not. But if I had been around, they'd remember. And surely if I was unconscious, someone would see. Was it possible that ...

That when I jumped into the story, I stopped existing in the real world?

The hairs on the back of my neck prickled.

Dad turned back to the stove. He switched the exhaust fan on and opened the window. When he moved, he didn't shuffle in the way I'd got used to. There was life in his steps. He was humming to himself.

The writing was still helping. He was almost back to his old self. I mean, his face was still lined and tired looking, and his back never used to be that hunched, and he wasn't exactly dancing. But he looked better.

When Dad finished cooking, he plated up the food. It was salmon with this crispy spicy coating and noodles with veg. I grabbed two empty plates and we took the meal through to the living room. I sat down, trying not to look at the urn on the mantelpiece. Dad flicked on the TV. There was nothing on, just chat shows and repeats. He cycled through the channels, then settled for an old detective drama from the seventies.

I didn't normally watch old TV, because it looked rubbish compared to modern stuff. Dad always used to go on about classic films like *Spartacus*. But when he put it on, I couldn't take it seriously. The fights looked like the ones you had with your friends when you were younger, using plastic swords and shields from the toy shop.

I didn't mind watching this, though. It was nice just to be spending time with Dad. I took a bite of food, hesitant after the market food in the story. But it tasted amazing. I tried to remember the taste of the burgers we made, but I couldn't. Everything was so muddled after all the jumps.

Six whole days. That was what I'd missed, living Dad's story.

Part of me wanted to shout, "It's not fair!" because they were hours and minutes I'd never get back. They were gone, snipped out of my life.

But an even bigger part of me wanted to keep jumping back into the story until I finished it. Because even though this situation wasn't fair on me, it wasn't fair on Dad either.

I might have lost days and hours and minutes, but he'd lost a year of his life like this. It was like he'd dug inside himself and only part of him was looking out at the world.

If I could help him, then everything would be worth it.

When the show ended, we stacked the plates on the coffee table and sat back, staring at the commercials. I wasn't really listening, but it didn't matter. It was nice just sitting there.

"We'll do it, you know," Dad said, out of nowhere.

I glanced across at him. He was looking up at the urn again. The afternoon sun dipped down behind the hedges outside, and where it hit the gold, it turned it a burning orange color.

"We'll set her free. Like she wanted. Scatter her ashes over the sea."

"I know," I said. "I know we will, Dad."

He attempted a smile but stopped halfway. I smiled back, but my mind was elsewhere now. I was thinking about the Darkness, thinking about the Marshal. Something still wasn't clicking. I was sure the City was dead, and I knew Jack's dad was still alive. But how could I contact him, without the radio tower?

I had to find a way. Maybe then, Dad would stay better. Maybe then, we *could* scatter Mum's ashes over the sea and put her back into the world again, instead of just talking about it. Otherwise we'd just be going round in these circles forever.

# 24

That night, Dad must have decided to write again, and I jumped. I pressed my fingers into my eyes against the swirling dizziness that wouldn't go away.

I was soaking wet, which meant I'd just come out of Cleansing. Iris and Dillon were with me too. We were squelching our way back to the main hall to get changed.

"Are you okay?" Iris asked.

"Yeah—just give me a second," I panted, blinking as everything came into focus.

We walked down the steps to the hall. The heart of the camp, carved into the belly of the King's College ruins. The TVs on the walls flickered with their commercials, talking about how great it was to be a Stormwalker, how important and heroic.

"Do you want to get some more lemon balm?"

"No, I'm all right . . ."

There was something I had to ask her . . .

"I've been thinking about what the Marshal said," I began, choosing the words carefully.

"What do you mean?" Iris said.

I lowered my voice, so Dillon wouldn't hear. "You know, in the church, after we heard that . . . that radio call . . ." But something about the look on her face made me falter.

Everything I'd been meaning to ask her crumbled away. There was no recognition there. A robot trundled closer, its camera whirring as it focused on us. Suddenly unnerved, I told Dillon I'd catch up with him in a bit, grabbed Iris and led her away, up the stairs to the market.

"Jack, what's going on? What radio call?"

"You were right there with me," I said. "After the Dreamless attacked, we ran back to camp and that call from Icarus 1—they said the City was—"

"What are you talking about? If we'd heard from Icarus 1, the whole camp would know about it," she said. "Are you sure you're feeling all right?"

My mouth hung open uselessly. Had she forgotten *everything*?


I couldn't stop thinking about it all through class the next morning. I barely listened when Mrs. Cloud showed off her latest finds—another set of objects scavenged by Iris. How could she have forgotten something so big? It didn't make sense.

"Jack?" someone said, startling me out of my thoughts.

"S-sorry?"

"Do you have any ideas on the topic?"

On the board at the back of the room were the words CD—Cylindrical Disk.

Below it, Mrs. Cloud had written: RECENT HISTORY.

I blinked, shaking my head. "Er . . . what, sorry?"

"We're listing the possible uses for this particular antique," she said, holding up a blank CD, which flashed silver in the light. "But if history and heritage don't concern you, then—"

"No," I said quickly, "I'm listening."

I scanned the board for some of the answers:

"Decoration"

"Sport"

"Place mats"

I'd only ever really used MP3s for my music, but we had loads of CDs in the house. I should have been surprised that they didn't know what they were used for, but after the Slinky and the tiddlywinks it didn't come as much of a shock.

"Er, music?" I suggested.

A few people burst out laughing, but Mrs. Cloud held up her hand for quiet. "That's actually not such a silly suggestion," she said, turning back to the board and writing Music down underneath the other ideas. "We have evidence, after all, that the pre-Darks had hard-copy technology for stories. Why not for music as well?"

After the lesson, I was walking up to the market square with Iris when it hit me.

She'd forgotten the radio call right after Cleansing. What was it they'd said? The pre-Darks used lemon balm to help alleviate the effects of Alzheimer's. Maybe they'd found a way to use it differently—to alter the mind in a different way.

What if the Darkness didn't affect your memory at all? What if the lemon balm—the thing that was supposed to be a *cure*—was making people forget? Making them think we'd only been here in camp for six months, making them forget the City was dead.

But then . . . how did *I* remember? I'd been through Cleansing too, hadn't I? There must be a reason for it. Maybe it was because I had two minds—Owen and Jack. When I plunged into Jack's thoughts, it was like I was watching them on TV, but once I'd seen his memories, they were *my* memories too. The lemon balm might have been enough to trick one of us, but not the other.

"Iris, what happens if you don't go to Cleansing?" I asked. I couldn't do this on my own. I needed her with me, but that couldn't happen if she forgot everything we learned.

"You can't not go to Cleansing," she said. "The LRP officers will find out. They'll take you to the Chamber."

"And what happens there again?"

"No one knows," Iris said, shuddering. "But I've seen two people go there, and neither of them came back."

We exchanged some caps for breakfast: some kind of cereal bar made from the millet we'd been Farming in the dry fields. It didn't taste too bad, but as soon as I ate it I needed a drink to wet my throat. Just as I was taking my plate back to the table, Quinn tapped me on the shoulder. James, the other officer from the hut, stood beside him, already piling food onto his plate.

"How are you holding up?" Quinn said.

"I'm all right." We hadn't spoken since the radio call. I'd barely seen him around at all. My first thought was that the Marshal was keeping him busier than ever after their argument. Or maybe Quinn just didn't want to give him an excuse to hurt me. But part of me was glad for it.

I'd trusted Quinn. But whatever the Marshal was covering up, he must have been in on it too. I wondered what he'd done to James, to make him forget about the radio call. I was sure he'd forgotten, just like Iris had forgotten—otherwise the whole camp would have known that Icarus 1 had made contact. Had he forced him through Cleansing too?

Quinn followed me back to where Iris was, and was just about to sit down when a female voice spurted from the radio on his belt.

"Quinn, you there?"

He took the radio and held it to his lips. "Talk to me."

"The Darkness," said the voice. "It's early again."

Quinn whispered something to James, who rushed off. Before long, a deep hum reverberated around us as the lights flickered back on.

I could see it now, in the distance. It spread across the horizon, oozing and bubbling in the sky. The sirens wailed as it got closer, low at first, then high and loud—a rolling wave of sound. It moved so fast. How could anyone get back in time if they were out now?

But even as I watched, other Stormwalkers who'd been out Hunting dashed through the barrier. The storm smashed into the protective bubble of light, faces gleaming, hissing and snarling with jet-black teeth.

"Quinn?" said the voice on the radio.

The sound cracked up. Quinn shook the radio, but the voice just stopped and started.

"I can't hear you. Sarah? Sarah, are you there?" Quinn tapped the radio with his free hand, held it as high as he could, but nothing happened.

Then there was a squeak and a whistling sound, and a new voice sputtered through.

"Flag is green," it said.

"Roger," said another voice, much quieter. More distant.

I glanced at Iris. Her eyes were wide. I didn't know what the man on the radio was talking about, but something about it sounded familiar . . .

Quinn frowned. He held the radio to his mouth, but stayed quiet. Then the radio fizzed again and Sarah came back.

"Quinn?" she said.

"I'm here."

"I thought I'd lost you."

"Did you hear that?" Quinn whispered urgently into the radio.

"Hear what?"

"Nothing," he said. "Don't worry." He noticed me listening and he started, as if he'd forgotten I was there. He moved away and lowered his voice. I strained to hear what he was saying, but it was no good. I looked at Iris, but she just shrugged.

All around us people darted through the square or down into the cellar. The storm raged and howled. I thought about the Dreamless, and wondered what happened to them when the Darkness was as thick as this.

*Flag is green* . . . Why did that seem so familiar? It sounded like some kind of code. And not just any code. It was the sort of thing you got on Call of Duty. But—

No, surely not.

On COD, it meant an air strike was going ahead.

It meant they were going to drop bombs.

*I've got to be wrong,* I thought. *Please let me be wrong.* Why would anyone want to bomb us? Unless . . . they'd sent three Icarus ships, hadn't they? Three camps, all trying to save the City. Maybe it *was* possible that one of them had been compromised, like Quinn said.

When we overheard that first radio call, the one from Icarus 1, they'd said they had an old airfield. They asked for our coordinates. Could they have found us from the snippet James gave?

*It's not real,* I told myself.

*It's just a story. It's all in Dad's head. He's making it up.*

But somehow I was here, really here. I'd been hurt when the Dreamless grabbed me, and if I could get hurt by that, then bombs would have no trouble ripping through me.

Quinn turned round, clipping the radio to his belt.

"Who were those voices?" I asked.

He hesitated. "I . . . er . . . I think we might have just intercepted a message from the City," he whispered, holding a hand up to cut short the excited squeals of the other Stormwalkers gathering nearby. "But don't get excited. I want to run it by the Marshal, to—"

He stopped.

Somewhere above us came a low whine, like an angry wasp, getting higher and faster.

"That's not the Darkness," he whispered.

"What is it?" Iris said, staring up into the impenetrable clouds.

"It sounds like a plane," I said. "I think it's . . . I think it's crashing."

"*Crashing?* How can you tell?"

"I've heard it before, on—" I was about to say "on the History Channel," but I stopped because if they didn't have that here then Quinn would definitely get suspicious. I closed my eyes, trying to pinpoint the noise. It sounded like it was over the park, heading toward Regent Street . . .

"No," I gasped.

It sounded like it was coming right for us.

A sharp screech split the sky above us, and the Darkness peeled away. In the gap where the clouds had been was a plummeting ball of fire. Adrenaline surged through me and cleared my head, letting a flood of memories rush free . . .

Once, before Mum died, she ran over a rabbit. She didn't mean to, it just darted out so quick that she couldn't stop. But the thing that stuck with me was that it froze just before we hit it, its eyes big and bright in the headlights. Why didn't it move? I'd never got it before.

But now I did, because this fireball was speeding straight toward us and I knew I needed to run, but I couldn't. My legs were rooted to the spot.

I blinked, and the spell broke.

An electric surge shot through me. "Come on," I said, grabbing Iris by the arm. My heart pumped a million miles an hour as I sprinted into the heart of the packed marketplace.

"Get out of the square!" I yelled.

She took up the cry with me. "Come on, everyone! *Move!*" But no one reacted. They were frozen by the sudden blaze in the night sky.

Iris dragged two kids back to the safety of a nearby shop. Following her lead, I grabbed the shirts of the nearest people to me and hauled them out of the way. Doing that finally snapped them out of whatever trance they were in, because all of a sudden everyone in the square shot out of the way as fast as they could. Glancing frantically around, I spotted another alleyway leading off the square. I darted down it, stealing a look back just in time to see others racing away in every direction, running as fast as they could—

*CRASH.*

The plane smashed through the chapel tower in an explosion of stone and dust. There was another bang, louder than a firework. The explosion shot up, up, up into the dark sky and the screeching of the storm joined in with the deafening boom and the never-ending wail of the sirens.

I crouched down, covering my ears, trying to shut out the noise.

A shockwave washed over us, a cloud of dust and grime, stinging my eyes and clogging my throat. Coughing and spluttering, I stood up and looked toward the wreckage, the explosion still ringing in my ears.

*Iris.*

I rushed inside to where she was kneeling with those other Stormwalkers. "Are you okay?" she asked, clambering to her feet and brushing dust off her rags.

"Yeah," I said. "I think so."

I turned around, covering my eyes against the searing flames. The thing in the market square didn't look like a plane. Not anymore. Tendrils of smoke rose from the engine. Halfway along, the body was crushed. It looked as if someone had snapped it in half. One of the wings was torn off, and the other was charred and blackened. Bits of propeller were bent out of shape, and the cockpit was smashed.

You could only tell what it was because of the tail, with its back wing still intact. But even through all that damage, I recognized it straightaway.

"It's a Spitfire," I whispered.

Just like the ones I'd seen at the air museum with Dad. Back when he used to take me. Before the drinking and the late nights, before the Longest Day.

People crept out of their hiding places now, mouths hanging open. Flames snapped and flickered around the wreckage, stopping anyone getting too close.

High in the sky, the Darkness gathered again, as if it'd never parted.

"Where's the pilot?" Iris whispered.

People took up the question, calling it out.

"Where's he gone? Where's the pilot?"

Maybe they'd parachuted out. But if they had, they'd have to have dropped through the Darkness. They'd have to have dropped through the raging storm.

I stepped back from the broken plane, staring up into the sky. Where the light grayed and dimmed above the rooftops, the dark clouds boiled and bubbled.

They kept asking that question—where's the pilot? But that wasn't the biggest question. I knew they didn't know what tiddlywinks was and they thought Slinkies were weapons, which probably meant they had no idea what a Spitfire was either.

But I did. And in this world, with everything so dead, with all the buildings broken and us just trying to survive every day in camp . . . where on earth had anyone got hold of a working Second World War plane?

# 25

The sky.

That was how I knew I was back in my world.

I was lying on my back, staring up at the sky, and it wasn't filled with screechy black clouds—it was blue and purple and orange where the sun started to dip down on the horizon. In the distance, streetlights painted the road in a misty orange glow.

I was wearing sweatpants and a T-shirt. The cold made the hairs on my arms stand on end. I tried to think back to what had happened before the jump, but the burned-out version of Cambridge rose up: the dusty murk of the cellar and the piercing glow of the electric lights.

I shook the fog from my head and sat up, reaching for my phone.

Four forty-three. Monday afternoon.

Had I missed another day? Every thought in my head burst into a million more and it was too hard to keep track of them all, too hard to think.

I could be anywhere. Holding my breath, I flicked through the phone until I got to the maps app and pressed the arrow that turned on the GPS.

*Come on, come on . . .*

Why did it never work when you really needed it to?

Finally the blank grid disappeared and the map flashed up. The blue dot blinked. I zoomed in on the name—Jesus Green.

The memory flashed again in my mind, the memory I'd tried a million times to forget. Because this was the park where she told me. This was where I found out about Mum having the L-word. I closed my eyes and hummed to myself, trying to get it out of my head.

A buzz from my phone made my eyes flash open. A text from Danny:

Missed you at training. Again.

Training! Our next game was just around the corner. And if I'd missed training, I might not even make the team.

I replied, asking Danny to meet me at my place, then ran home as fast as I could. Danny was waiting outside the front door by the time I got there. He frowned when he saw me.

"Where've you been?" he said.

"You're never going to believe me."

Danny followed me to the kitchen and watched as I gulped down a whole pint of water, pushing the dust and the Darkness further and further away.

"Wow!" Danny said. "Thirsty much?"

We found Dad in the living room, watching football and drinking a beer.

"All right, Owen?" he said. "All right, Danny? How are your mum and dad?"

"Fine," Danny said.

"Got a big match this week, eh? Reckon you'll be able to take them?"

"I think so," Danny said, his eyes locking onto mine. "As long as we all show up."

I shot him a look that said, *Please don't say anything,* because if Dad found out I wasn't at the game last week it could ruin everything. He'd stop writing completely, and then I'd never get to finish the story for him, and he'd never get better. Dad looked as if he was going to ask more, but something in the match caught his attention and he turned away.

I led Danny up to my room, just hoping Dad would start writing soon, because if he didn't, I wouldn't be able to show Danny what I was talking about. And I needed him to see. It wouldn't be the same without showing him.

"Look, I'm really sorry," I said, sitting down on the beanbag. It felt like the kind of conversation you had to sit down for. The kind that made your legs wobbly with nerves. Danny sat on the floor. "I didn't mean to miss the game last week. I promise."

He scuffed the carpet, then looked up at me. "So where were you?"

"Danny," I said, already dreading how insane it was going to sound. "Dad's writing a new story. And I'm . . . I keep getting transported into it. Into the world of his book."

"You're what?" he said. For a second he stared at me in disbelief. Then he burst out laughing.

"I'm being serious," I said. "I need you to believe me."

Danny charged on as if I hadn't even spoken. "You missed football when you said you'd be there. You're never in lessons, either—"

"I am!"

"Not all the time," he said, cutting across me. "Like today. Where were you then?"

"Danny—"

"I didn't even realize you were gone until PE. It was like I forgot you existed."

"*Exactly*," I said, raising my voice now. "Danny, I know it sounds weird, but . . ."

But he was remembering now . . .

I'd never stopped to wonder why. How come he realized I wasn't at school, when Dad and the teachers didn't? It was always around football. He remembered when I missed the match, and just now he said he'd remembered after PE.

Ever since we were tiny kids, we'd dreamed of playing for Cambridge together. Maybe it was just too different without me there.

Or maybe . . . maybe it was because all this time, I *wanted* him to know.

Right now, though, all I wanted to do was shout at him, but I couldn't, because I knew how ridiculous it sounded. There was no such thing as getting written into a story. There was no such thing as living the pages. But somehow it was happening to me. Somehow I kept teleporting out of this world and into the one Dad created. I picked up the Play-Station controller, flipping it around to have something to do with my hands.

"Tell me the truth," he said. "You owe me that."

"I have—"

"You can't do it, can you? Even now, all you do is lie."

"I'm *not* lying!"

How could I make him see? If only Dad were writing, and I'd be able to show him whatever happened to me. But Dad was still watching football, and it would be on for ages yet.

Danny shook his head. He got up and moved to the door. "Danny!" I tried, but he turned and strode off along the landing.

"So much for the dream team," he muttered, storming downstairs.

I heard the bang of the front door. I stood there, wondering how it had all gone so wrong. Danny's words echoed in my mind. *All you do is lie.*

I flopped back onto the beanbag, alone in the silence.

# 26

The next time I woke up in the story, it was too hard to concentrate.

I tried to listen to Mrs. Cloud in the morning class, tried to contribute when she talked about one object or another. I even jumped into Jack's thoughts to answer a question about the City. But the whole time, I kept picturing Danny, and the look on his face as he backed away.

*All you do is lie.*

It wasn't like he hated me.

He was disappointed, and that made it a million times worse.

How much time had I missed now, living in this wasteland? I wanted to help Dad, and I knew that if I could figure out what the Marshal was doing, if I could solve the mystery, if I could somehow reunite Jack with his family, then I could finish the story and maybe Dad would get better.

But the longer I spent here, the more time I missed with Danny, and I wasn't sure how much more I could take. If he just believed me . . . if he just listened, maybe it would be better. But as it stood, he didn't feel like my best friend. He felt more and more like a stranger.

After class, our group walked toward the farm, ready to tend to the vegetables and the seeds. Iris tried to talk to me, but she stopped when she saw how distracted I was.

We were just passing the market square when something made me freeze. I gazed around, trying to piece it together. What was I missing? Had I skipped some of the story, like the days that vanished back in real life?

Then I realized . . .

Out in the square, beside the crumbling remains of the shattered clock tower, was—

Well, nothing.

"The plane," I whispered.

"What plane?" said Iris.

I was already walking toward the patch of dirt where it had crashed, but now my heart skipped a beat and I whirled round, facing her.

"What?" she said. "Is this another one of your—"

"Iris," I said slowly. "The plane. The one that crashed right here . . ."

She shook her head blankly.

"How could you forget?" I demanded. How could this be happening again? First the radio call, and now this? I spun back round, questioning myself now, but the clock tower had been intact before, one of the only whole things about this wasteland. And it was scattered across the square just as it had been when—

"What did we do when I was last here?" I said.

"I don't understand. You're . . . you're always here."

"What did we do yesterday then? What happened? Can you remember?"

"The same as we do every day," she said. "We went to class, we Farmed and Hunted. And then we went Stormwalking and went to Cleansing."

*No*, I thought, *no, no, no* . . .

"Dillon," I called, waving him over despite Iris's protests. "The crash. Tell me you remember the crash. Yesterday, before—"

"What are you talking about?" he said.

I shook my head, but I couldn't get my thoughts in order. I couldn't piece it together. My stomach felt so heavy. *What's going on?* I thought, the question getting louder and louder and bigger and bigger until it was the only thing on my mind.

"I've got to find Quinn," I said.

Now it was Iris's turn to look confused.

"Jack, we've got to stick to the timetable—"

But I was already running off, rubble pinging from my feet and dust clouding up into the electric glow of the wasteland air. The way Quinn spoke when the radio call came in. It was like he'd expected it. Like he'd heard it before. He didn't panic when he heard them say the City was dead. And then there was the way he acted, after the crash . . .

The crash that Iris and Dillon couldn't remember.

Across the crunching, narrow paths I ran, choking on the dust. High above, there was a whoosh and a sizzling crack as the Darkness thundered into the dome of light. High, piercing screeches rang out a final time, and then the storm retreated, giving way to the grayness of the day and a pale-orange sun on the horizon.

The protective dome hummed and disconnected. I spotted an LRP team on the edge of camp, gathered around Quinn's truck. As soon as the storm disappeared, the engine grumbled, loud and clear across the ruins.

Quinn knew about the radio call. He hadn't forgotten that, and if he hadn't forgotten that, he might not have forgotten the plane crash either. "Quinn!" I yelled, trying to make myself heard above the noise.

He didn't look up. They were going to speed off, and then there'd be no one left to talk to.

"Quinn!" I shouted again, rotten wood and worn-down bricks crumbling beneath my feet as I legged it closer.

At last, one of the other officers turned back and saw me. He leaned in through the window and said something to Quinn. The engine cut off and the driver's door opened. Quinn poked his head out, waiting for me.

I skidded to a stop, each breath of dusty air stinging my throat.

"Are you all right?" he said.

"Yeah," I said, my voice dry and raspy. Now that I was here, I didn't know what to say. Well, I did, but I didn't know *how* to say it. I mean . . .

Quinn must have seen the look on my face because he said something to his team, then got out of the truck.

"What is it?" he said, leading me out of earshot of the others. "The sun's out. We need every minute we can get."

I took a deep breath and looked him in the eyes. "The plane wreck. It's gone."

Quinn gripped my arm hard. He dragged me to the side of the camp, away from the well-trodden paths. "What did you say?" he whispered.

I blinked groggily. "The plane," I said again. "It's gone."

Quinn's face was so close now, I could smell buttery corn on his breath.

"How do you know about that?" He lowered his voice as a group of kids swept past. "When was the last time you went to Cleansing?"

I knew it! I knew I was right. So the Marshal *was* hiding something from us.

"Jack . . . no one . . . no one's supposed to remember."

"That's not the only thing," I said. "I remember the radio call too. Iris doesn't. The lemon balm made her forget, didn't it? Is that what's happened to everyone else? He's drugging them or something?"

Quinn's head was shaking. His mouth worked, open and closed, but no words came out. A robot trundled by, and it must have jolted him to his senses, because he gripped me by both arms and dragged me away again.

"Listen to me," he growled, his voice so low I could barely hear it. "Do not mention that plane again. If you do . . ." He trailed off, turning to face the gray horizon.

"Quinn, what's going on?"

"We can't talk about this. Not now. It's too dangerous. He has eyes everywhere, and—"

He cut off suddenly, and I spun around to see Mrs. Cloud walking past with another kid, their arms full of books and age-browned photos.

"Who? The Marshal? It's true, isn't it? The City's dead." Jack's thoughts bubbled over as I said it. Images of his dad and brother filled my mind. "We're supposed to be heroes. We're supposed to be saving them, but they're dead, and no one knows about it because you won't tell them. Why won't you tell them?" Hot tears burned behind my eyes.

"Jack—"

"If it's only the Icarus projects left, we need to go to them. That was . . . that was my dad on the radio," I said, almost slipping up. It was weird calling him *my* dad when I knew my real dad, Owen's dad, was back home writing this.

"*Jack,*" Quinn hissed, and my shoulders slumped as all the energy leaked out of me. "Listen to me. You're not supposed to know this—any of it. Do you hear me? I don't know how you do know it, but if you don't keep quiet you'll get yourself killed, or worse. Who have you told about this?"

"No one. Just . . . well, I was with Iris when I realized . . ."

He sighed heavily, and glanced around again. "Don't mention it to anyone," he said. "Forget you ever saw it. And whatever you do, don't go looking for it, okay? I need you to promise me."

*Don't go looking for what?* I thought.

The plane wreck? Did that mean it was still around here, somewhere?

"I told your dad I'd look after you. I promised him I'd keep you safe. And I've tried, Jack. I've really tried, because I thought that . . . I thought that if we could ride it out, there would be another way. But I can't protect you if you go digging around. Promise me you won't."

Didn't he see? If the Marshal was covering up evidence of the City, if he was hiding communication from Icarus 1, I *had* to go digging. I had to find a way to show the Marshal up.

I had to find a way to prove it, so I could get back to Jack's family.

Quinn's face was set. It was chalk white, and draining ever whiter by the second. I'd never seen him like this before. I couldn't tell him what I really thought.

"All right," I said, the tiniest glimmer of an idea forming in the back of my mind. Maybe there *was* a way I could get through to Jack's dad after all. I crossed my fingers behind my back. "All right, I promise—I won't go looking for anything."

He didn't reply. Just kept staring at me.

No, not at me.

Staring *behind* me.

I whirled around, and my breath caught—

He was walking toward us, flanked by LRP officers.

"Well, well, well," said the Marshal. "Shall we go for a walk, old friend?"

# 27

"Quinn!" I called, trying to fight my way toward him—

But I was already tumbling back . . .

Falling, falling, falling, until with a sudden jolt I found myself in my bedroom, staggering into the desk. I held on to it to keep myself steady, breathing fast.

How much had the Marshal heard?

I thumped the wood in frustration. If Quinn was in trouble, it was all my fault, wasn't it? I was the one who went to him. I was the one who dragged him away from his job. He would never have said any of that stuff if it wasn't for me.

I checked my phone quickly. I hadn't missed another day, but it was late.

The sky outside was a thick dark blue. Stars twinkled above the black silhouettes of trees.

I climbed into bed, even though I didn't feel tired at all. My heart was still thumping hard.

Even after Jack's thoughts vanished, I couldn't stop thinking about the story. Jack's dad was telling the truth, wasn't he? The City was dead. But Iris had forgotten all about the radio call and now the plane had been cut right out of her mind too. All because of the Marshal.

It was only me. I was on my own.

Somehow I had to prove what the Marshal was doing. I had to contact Icarus 1. And I thought I knew how I could do it. If I could just find the wreckage of the plane, then maybe I could find its black box. It would be just like that show on TV—I could use the location device inside it to make contact with the other camp.

I fell back against the pillow, sighing heavily.

I wished I could talk to Danny about it. Whenever we played two-penny football in Math and the teacher caught us messing around and asked us an impossible question on the spot, he would always get it right. That was Danny—he was brilliant at problem solving.

But I couldn't get Danny's help, could I?

As I lay there, staring at all the football posters on the walls, his words burned their way back into my mind, like they'd been branded onto it.

*All you do is lie.*

My best friend thinking I was lying to his face was almost as bad as the Darkness. At least in the story I knew I was safe as long as I stayed within the light. At school the next day, every time I looked up I could see how upset he was, and there was no protective barrier against that.

I tried to talk to him at roll call, but he just moved away, and with all our class staring at us, I felt too embarrassed to chase after him.

He sat apart from me in every lesson, and it wasn't until PE, when we played hockey, that I finally managed to grab him.

His eyes widened as I forced him back toward the empty goal at the end of the lesson. Everyone else was walking off to dump their equipment in the shed.

"What're you going to do, hit me?" he said, eyeing the stick in my hands.

I was gripping it so hard my knuckles were white. I dropped it quickly, and it clattered on the Astroturf.

"Just leave it—"

"Listen, Danny, *I promise you on my dad's life* . . ." I hesitated, face frozen, waiting for him to react. His mouth hung open. Because no matter how much he thought I was lying, he knew I'd never joke about that. "I'm . . . I'm getting written into his story," I said.

His mouth opened and closed wordlessly. He frowned, then rubbed his short black hair and shook his head in confusion.

"But . . . that's impossible," he said, and the words came out so quiet.

"I know. But you have to believe me. It's true. Whenever he writes, I wake up in his story. Like I've teleported. Like I've been dragged inside the pages. I get sucked out of this world and into his one. Danny, it's horrible. There's this storm called the Darkness, and it's alive. You can hear it screeching in the sky. Everyone thinks they're saving the City, but they're not. There's this man called the Marshal, and he's covering it all up. But if he finds out I know . . ."

I trailed off, shuddering at the thought of what might happen.

Danny was still shaking his head.

I needed him to believe me. I needed him to see.

"Come round again after school," I said. "I'll . . . I'll show you."


Now all I had to do was make sure Dad started writing.

When the bus dropped us off at the end of the road, we walked quickly back to my house, thinking up a plan.

"I'll hide the TV remote," I said.

"And we can cut the Internet off too," Danny said, his lips twitching. I felt a flutter of excitement. Even if he didn't completely believe me, for now at least, he was back on my side.

We hurried up the drive, and slipped into the house as quietly as possible. In the hallway, I listened out for any sound of movement inside the house.

There—

In the kitchen. The fridge opening. The clink of glass bottles.

"Quickly," I whispered.

We moved into the living room as fast as we dared, trying to keep quiet. Our socks were silent on the wooden floor. I grabbed the remote and shoved it into the inside pocket of my school jacket. Danny went to the corner of the room and unplugged the Internet cable, then slotted it back in just enough so it still looked connected.

"Come on!" I urged him, rushing back to the hall now just as the kitchen door opened.

I chucked my bag down, pretending we'd just arrived. Dad appeared in the doorway, holding a beer. He blinked.

"All right, lads? Didn't hear you come in."

"Hi, Mr. Smith," Danny said.

"Good day at school?" he asked, moving past the study and through to the living room.

"It was okay," we said together.

We waited round the corner as Dad sat down. He glanced around for the remote, then scratched his head. I looked at Danny. He winked back at me. When I turned back to the living room, Dad was feeling down the sides of the sofa.

"Where the hell did I put it?" he muttered.

Then he sighed heavily, and stood up—

This was it!

*Please start writing*, I thought desperately.

But Dad was going over to the TV. He crouched beside it, moving his fingers along the side of the screen. Of course! How could I forget? He didn't need the remote. The TV flashed on.

Dad slouched back to the sofa and flopped down.

I turned to Danny, thinking quickly. Then I dug inside my jacket pocket and pulled out the remote. Pointing it at the TV, I pressed the power button, and the screen went off. Trying not to laugh, I ducked back around the corner.

Dad muttered something about technology being rubbish these days, and got up to turn the TV on again, but as soon as he did, I switched it off. Trying to keep a straight face, I led Danny through and sat down.

"Blinking thing must be on the way out," Dad said.

"Maybe it's a sign," I said. "Less TV, more writing."

Dad chuckled. "You sound like my counselor," he said.

He gave up trying to get the TV to turn on and stood up, walking in the direction of his study. Danny and I sat there for a few moments longer, then went upstairs to my room.

"Do you think it'll work?" he said.

"It has to."

I told him all about the story as quickly as I could, from the Darkness to the creepy Dreamless living out in the storm, to the plane crash. I told him about the Marshal, how I suspected him of covering up the death of the City, but that I didn't know why. I told him how I thought the writing was helping Dad to get better, but that didn't mean I *wanted* to miss the football.

"I can do both," I said. "Help Dad, *and* get through to the next stage of the championship."

"Let's just say you are telling the truth," Danny went on, although he sounded as if he still thought it was the craziest thing he'd ever heard. "How . . . how does it even happen?"

"I don't know, I just—"

That was when I felt it.

The tug in my gut, the twisting and churning.

"It's happening," I said suddenly, standing up and gripping the bed frame as the world whirled around me. "It's happening right now. He must be writing me in!"

Danny's mouth moved as if he was talking, but no sound came out. The blood rushed in my ears and all I could hear was whooshing—a constant whipping roar.

"It's happening!" I yelled above the noise. "Can you see it?"

In a second I was going to be back there, I could feel it.

"I don't want to go!" I called, but my voice got snatched away by the roaring wind.

My stomach flipped and churned, but I tried to fight it. I had to fight it. I knew I was the one who *wanted* Dad to write, but only to show Danny. I didn't think about actually going back. If I didn't fight it, who knew when I'd be me again? I'd miss the next match too and then Danny would never forgive me.

My eyes streamed with the effort. I threw my hands up, trying to find Danny in the chaos. But he was already turning away. It was as if he'd lost sight of me altogether.

*No.*

I clenched my teeth, desperate to fight it, to prevent the jump . . .

And then it stopped. The whirling, the rushing, the noise. The only sound was the blood pumping in my ears and Danny rummaging through my collection of video games.

"Did you see?" I asked, breathing heavily.

He jolted in surprise. "Owen!" he said. "What's . . . what's going on?"

"You were watching. You were looking right at me."

His face scrunched up the way it did in Science when Mr. Herring asked a difficult question.

"What?" he said. "No. No . . ."

He shook his head. His eyes dropped to the floor, to the TV, to the collection of games.

"What do you remember?" I asked, thinking back to the way Dad looked so lost when I talked to him about the missing days. Could Danny really have forgotten already?

"I . . ."

"We were just here, talking."

"Yeah," he said, shaking his head in disbelief. "Yeah. It's like . . . it's there in my head, but it's not. The last thing I remember is talking to you, and then it's just blurry."

Something yanked my stomach. "It's happening again!"

"Yeah," Danny whispered slowly. "Your whole body's sort of . . . electric."

The tug got worse and Danny's voice was lost in a swirl of color. It was like when you went bodyboarding and you were riding a wave, getting faster and faster, and then it pulled you under. For a second you'd be gulping air with bubbles exploding around you and everything so bright.

The other Cambridge crept into my mind, the dirt and the dust and the damp air, but I shoved it back. Jack's voice rose up, but I ignored it.

*I'm Owen Smith.*

I pictured my room and held it there, refusing to let go.

And then there was quiet. There was quiet and Danny just standing there.

"Owen," he said, looking confused.

"I'm here," I panted. Fighting the jump had left my legs weak. I fell into my gaming chair, breathing way too fast.

He chewed his lips. He stepped back, shaking his head.

"You did it again, didn't you?"

"Yeah."

That explained why Dad and the teachers at school never remembered anything when I got back. It was like something blurred their thoughts, muddling them up and hiding them.

"But—I mean, where did you go? You're still here. I thought you said—"

"I fought it. I didn't go anywhere. I almost did, but I . . . I stopped it."

Danny was still staring at me as if I was an alien, but I couldn't really blame him. It wasn't every day your friend disappeared before your eyes. I clutched my stomach, where the tug started. There was an echo of it there—a slight twinge where my hand touched the skin.

"That's so cool." Danny's face relaxed for the first time. He was still shaking his head slowly, but he was smiling broadly now. "It's like . . . like you're a superhero or something."

I laughed, but inside I wasn't laughing. I wasn't like a superhero at all. Superheroes saved hundreds of people every day. And they didn't get scared. But I didn't know how to save the people in Dad's story. And I was scared now . . .

Scared of jumping back into the story and missing more of my own life.

And, now that I thought about it, scared that something might happen because I didn't.

# 28

The next day, I fought the jump again.

It was easier this time.

I found I just had to focus on something so much that it was all I could see, even when I closed my eyes. Like the work on the board at school, or Chris Matthews flicking ink over Bradley White's shirt, or the way a potato chip bag drifted across the courtyard when the wind picked up.

I stared and stared and clenched all the muscles in my stomach and focused the whole time, and the tug stopped.

At breakfast, Dad had mentioned how hard it had been to write last night. I kept expecting him to barge into a lesson today yelling, "I NEED TO WRITE!" But he didn't know about me getting written in and there was no way he could know about me fighting it.

Part of me felt bad, because the writing was helping. I knew it was. I'd seen it in so many different ways. But with the game tomorrow, I wanted to stick around, just for one more day. I wanted to be me—Owen Smith—not inside Jack's head in the wasteland.

All through school the guilt got worse. I barely talked on the bus, and even though I tried to listen as Danny told me about Westfield's tactics, I kept zoning out.

When I got back, I hesitated outside the front door.

*That's weird*, I thought. There were no lights on. I opened the door and called out, but there was no answer. Quiet—the whole house was so quiet. I even checked out in the shed, but Dad wasn't there either. Where was he? I flicked on my phone, but there weren't any messages. There were no notes left round the house. Something squirmed inside my stomach now, but it wasn't the tug of Dad's writing. What if something bad had happened and it was all my fault?

When I was sure the house was empty, I chucked my bag down and went upstairs, loading up FIFA to take my mind off it. But I kept the volume low, so I would know if Dad came back.

Before long, I heard the *crunch-crunch-crunch* of footsteps on the drive.

I dropped the controller and rushed across the landing to the window.

He was walking up the driveway slowly, like his legs couldn't be bothered to work. When he finally unlocked the door, he just stood there cast in shadow by the light from the house.

In Art we'd started doing pen-and-ink drawings, where you used white paper and the darkest ink and nothing else. You couldn't see any features, but that was what made it look so good.

That was what Dad looked like now. A pen-and-ink drawing.

I tried to imagine what was going through his head. I wondered if he pictured Mum like I did, pictured her smiling face in his mind. Maybe she was fading for him too.

Finally Dad walked inside. I heard his footsteps trailing into the living room. I didn't know whether to go downstairs or not. He might not have been in the mood to talk. But I couldn't just leave him.

Taking a deep breath, I walked down to the living room, and curled up next to him on the sofa. We sat there in silence, not saying anything at all. He stroked my hair and hugged me close. He smelled of beer and that stale smell you got in pubs sometimes, but I didn't mind.

The starlight twinkled on Mum's urn, and as I watched it, I had to talk about her.

"Dad?" I said. "What is something you loved about Mum?"

He cleared his throat and I thought he was going to speak, but he didn't reply.

"I loved her smile," I said, the words bubbling over now. "When she saw me, no matter how bad her day had been, when she saw me she smiled and—"

"That's enough," Dad said. His eyes were red and rimmed with tears. When he blinked, one trickled down the side of his face. He swiped at it with his hand. "I can't do this. Not now."

"I just thought—"

"I can't, Owen. Not yet." He sighed, and took a deep, shuddering breath.

I sat back on the sofa, listening to the occasional drone of traffic outside the house, and the steady breathing of Dad, beside me. A sharp snort told me he'd fallen asleep.

A few days ago, he'd said he would come to watch our second game. But the game was tomorrow, and I got the impression he wouldn't be on the sideline again.

"One more day," I said. "Just give me this match, and then I'll finish the story."

It was amazing how easy it was to tell him about it when I knew he couldn't hear me.


After school the next day, I waited for Danny outside the sports center.

It was the day of the big match, and . . . I crossed my fingers just in case, for extra good luck—I was actually going to get to play in it! I hadn't felt the tug all day.

I swatted away the guilty feeling that twisted its way among the nerves. Dad had been so quiet last night, and it was all my fault, wasn't it? If I hadn't fought the jump, if I'd let him get on and write, he'd still be smiling.

I hoped he was okay—but I forced myself to focus, just for now. Just a few more hours.

The scout was already here.

Bradley White had seen him arrive and the news spread round school in minutes.

All that talk of the quarter finals had been a bluff. Maybe he'd wanted to catch us out, to see how we played naturally.

Normally when 3:15 hit, kids couldn't wait to get home, but now they crowded the courtyards, kicking footballs around, and marching in groups onto the field.

It was going to be the biggest crowd we'd had all season. And because I fought the jump, I was going to get to play. As long as I could keep it under control.

I closed my eyes, trying not to think about what would happen if Dad wrote me into the story in the middle of a game. No one had noticed so far. Danny forgot even when he watched me vanish. But I'd never had a crowd see me disappear before.

"All right?" Danny said, striding toward me.

"All right," I said.

Now that the bell had gone, my stomach bubbled with nerves. Everyone called them butterflies, but they didn't feel like butterflies. Butterflies were light and airy and they didn't flap their wings very fast. This felt more like a nest full of hummingbirds waking up and flapping their wings at the speed of light.

"I've been thinking about what you said," Danny said, pulling me to one side.

"What do you mean?"

"The story," he said, leaning in so no one could hear us. "You know, getting in contact with that other camp.

You can't do it in front of the others, so that rules out the radio. But maybe you don't need to use the radio anyway."

We were at the changing room door now, and Mr. Matthews was beckoning us in. Normally around a game Danny was focused on nothing but the match. Even *away* from the game, he barely talked about anything else.

"The plane," he said, as if that explained everything. "It'll have one of those things, won't it? Those black boxes. Whatever it is they use to track it. Maybe if you find it, you could get them to contact you."

"That's what I was thinking," I said, smiling widely.

I thought back to Quinn, telling me not to go looking for the wreck. But I had to, didn't I? If I got the black box, I could take it to the hill when we went out Hunting. Take it right up to the highest point, where the radio tower was.

Mr. Matthews waved at us again, blasting his whistle. We jogged inside and joined the rest of the team in the dressing room. Music played from someone's phone, and the clattering of studs filled the room as we changed into our uniforms and slipped our cleats on.

"You know the drill," Mr. Matthews said. "They're a good team, these lot. They hammered us last time, but it's a brand-new game. It's 0–0. And we've got the home advantage now. Don't think about the aggregate, and definitely don't think about the academy scout on the sideline. Just think about getting that ball in the back of the net."

He went through the starting eleven, and everyone clapped as the names got read out. Most games, we played a 4-4-1-1 formation. I was the number ten, behind Danny up front.

Mr. Matthews read through the defenders and the midfielders, then—

Danny stared at me. The whole team was staring at me. Mr. Matthews's voice rang in my ears, but it wasn't my name. He didn't call my name.

"Sorry, Owen," he said, clanking over to the door in his cleats. "I'm not sure when it was, but I've got down here that you missed training. You know the rules. No training, no start. Even for you."

*No . . .* I had to play!

A ball of fire formed inside my chest, burning and burning and getting so hot I thought it might explode. He didn't call my name. He *always* called my name, and now I was on the bench for the biggest game of my life. It wasn't just the academy scout I was worried about.

Dad had said he'd come too.

I scanned the crowd as we headed onto the field, but I couldn't see him anywhere.

Maybe he was running late. He'd probably be here in a bit.

"He'll put you on," Danny muttered. "He's got to."

Then the players lined up on the pitch, and Danny ran to the center circle. I shoved my hands in my pockets against the cold. It got dark so early now that the flood-lights were on, and I looked up at them, wondering what would be happening in the story if I'd jumped instead of fighting it.

Westfield was a good team. Their players were big and strong—the kind of kids who looked like Year 9s even when they were still in Year 7. They started the game confidently, and why wouldn't they? They had a 4–1 lead in the bag.

They snatched the ball quickly and almost broke through, but Scott Charles slid in and made the tackle. He passed it out to Aaron on the wing, and all of a sudden we were away.

Aaron sped down the sideline and Westfield couldn't get back in time . . .

"Cross it!" I yelled, running along the edge of the pitch. "Get it to Danny!"

Aaron swerved it in, and Danny rose up and connected with a perfect header.

Just like that we were 1–0 up. Two more and we'd be through to the next round!

The goal must have stung Westfield, because they soon cranked up the pressure. I was still annoyed at Mr. Matthews for not letting me play, but I quickly forgot about it because I didn't have a second to think. By half-time they'd had most of the ball and we'd barely got back inside their half.

At the break, Mr. Matthews brought round a bowlful of sliced oranges. As he moved past, he nodded at me and said, "Warm up." An electric surge shot through me. I glanced over at the home crowd again. I could see the scout making notes on his clipboard. But there was still no sign of Dad.

I tried not to get too disappointed, but I really thought he'd come this time. Where was he? Was it me? Was it because I fought the tug of the story?

I jumped up and down to get warm, shaking the thoughts from my head. As soon as this match was over, I'd stop fighting the tug, but for now I needed to focus.

This was it. I was playing in front of the academy scout.

I lined up right beside Danny when the whistle blew. Westfield kicked off and tried to keep possession, but Danny rushed in to pressure them and I scampered round, cutting off their options.

Frustration bit and they went for a long ball—and that was when we struck.

Dom intercepted the pass and threaded it through to me and I ran at them, just ran without caring. The change of pace must have thrown them off guard, because I got by one and then past two and a lane opened up for me to slot in Danny . . .

The crowd roared as he latched onto the pass and tapped the ball past the keeper to send us 2–0 up. I glanced across, dodging excited thumps and bear hugs. Mr. Matthews was grinning like mad. The scout looked right at me, then scribbled something on his pad.

But we still needed one more.

Down by two, Westfield started to panic. You could tell by their quick, snappy passes. They wanted to control the game, but their plan had fallen apart and now they didn't know how to react.

Aaron intercepted a ball and played me onside down the right wing. I quickly looked up, trying to find Danny, but they had him well marked. Time was running out. I had to do something.

The defender lunged at me with an outstretched leg, and I dinked the ball past him and ran round and into the box. Everything moved so slowly now. The keeper crouched low, watching me with wide eyes. Another defender was closing in. People were calling out, shouting different things, but I didn't hear any of it.

I didn't even think—just reacted.

I rolled the ball left, past the second defender, and smashed it with my left foot.

It was my wrong foot, but I didn't have time for anything else.

The ball rocketed into the left post—

It ricocheted—

And rolled across the line. It was in. It was in!

An explosion of noise erupted and the crowd ran onto the pitch. Students and teammates and even one or two teachers rushed on to mob me and I fell tumbling back onto the grass.

Crushing pain shot through me every time someone leapt onto the pile, but I didn't care.

"You've done it!" they said.

"We've won! We've won!"

The referee's whistle trilled five long blasts as he tried to get everyone under control. I didn't know how long it was before I could finally get back up. I brushed the grass off my elbows and straightened out my uniform, and my cheeks burned from the giant smile that wouldn't leave my face.

The game got back underway, but before long the ref blew the whistle again—three sharp blasts. The cheers rang out louder than before. I stood there in the middle of the pitch, taking long, deep breaths, letting it all soak in.

"We're through!" Danny yelled, dragging me into a hug. I winced at the sharp pain in my ribs. "Well played, mate. Really well played!"

"You too," I said. "Talk about a good header."

He shoved me away, ruffling my hair.

The school chant started up in the background, ringing out over the emptying field.

"Lads," called Mr. Matthews, and I turned to see him standing there beside the scout. He beckoned us over. "There's someone here who wants a word with you."

I glanced up at the sky, wondering if Mum was up there somewhere. Wondering if she saw. Wondering if she had anything to do with it.

There were no hummingbirds in my stomach anymore.

Just a tight ball of excitement shuddering away, ready to burst.

# 29

All the way home, my stomach squirmed.

Trials at Cambridge Academy! If only Dad had come to the match. It would have been the perfect game to see. I knew I'd been annoyed about not starting, but the second half was brilliant.

I rushed to the door and nearly dropped the key. I couldn't wait to tell Dad.

"Dad?" I called.

There was no reply.

I called out again, but there was still no answer.

I moved through the house, opening every door, my excitement draining with every step. He wasn't in the living room. The study was empty too. In the kitchen, there was a plate covered in toast crumbs and a mug with some coffee left in it, but no Dad.

I walked out through the dining room and on my way I noticed the back door was open.

Dad never left the back door open. My heart quickened. Were we being robbed? Was there someone upstairs? I thought of my TV and my PlayStation and almost went up to check they were still there, but something stopped me.

There was banging outside.

I hesitated for a second. Was it Dad out there, or someone else?

It sounded like the noise was coming from the shed.

The shed where all Mum's paintings were.

I slipped out through the back door. The shed light was on. I could see someone through the nearest window and I knew right away it was Dad. He lifted something up—a painting, it had to be—and chucked it out into the garden.

My throat dried up. It wasn't just one painting on the grass. It was three—now four, now five—all piled up one on top of the other. What was he doing? Why would he throw them around like that? For months he'd never set foot in there. Neither of us had. Not until the other day.

And now he was wrecking it. He was wrecking everything.

"No!" I shouted, but it didn't come out like a shout, it came out like a squeak.

My knees quivered. A few minutes ago I was dancing in the clouds, but now the game felt like it'd happened to someone else.

Dad chucked out another painting. He slammed the door. I imagined the wood rattling, the dust and cobwebs shaking free. He grabbed the nearest picture and smashed it on his knee, throwing the broken fragments into the bushes.

"No!" I yelled again, and it was louder this time.

My legs caught fire and I ran. Dad glanced up, but didn't stop. He was already reaching for the next painting.

I needed to stop him.

I *had* to stop him.

But I wasn't going to get there in time.

It happened in slow motion. He lashed out with his foot, kicking right through a canvas.

*No . . .*

Didn't he realize? Didn't he care?

"What are you doing?" I cried. I grabbed his arms and pulled him back, willing him to stop. "Those are Mum's!"

"Get off me," he spat, shrugging me off.

He reached for another painting, but I jumped in his way. He stopped, glaring at me. His face was set, like a stone mask.

"What the hell are you doing?" I said. I tried to hold his gaze, but his eyes burned into me.

"Get out of my way, Owen."

Behind him the twisted, tangled remains of the paintings were scattered in the weeds and the mud. There were flashes of color on some of the larger bits of canvas. I could just make out a few stars and something blue that could have been a wave.

"Mum painted these," I said, but it was the wrong thing to say, because his eyes narrowed and he barged past me and snatched another painting.

I grabbed hold of it but Dad yanked and pulled and even though I was gripping with everything I had, the canvas was slipping out of my grasp.

"Let . . . *go!*" Dad said, ripping it out of my hands and chucking it into the bushes. He kicked at it, but swung his leg so hard that he missed. It was almost funny, except there was nothing humorous about the look on his face.

He knelt down, pressing his knuckles hard into the grass.

"Why?" he said. He wasn't shouting now. It came out more like a whimper. "*Why?*" That was all he said, as his fists dug deeper and deeper into the mud.

"You're scaring me," I said. This wasn't my dad. This was an animal—a wild thing.

"*Dad,*" I said, louder this time.

Finally he looked up, breathing heavily. He held his head in his hands. His knuckles were smeared with dirt and there was grime under his fingernails.

"Why?" he said again.

He was shaking, his shoulders heaving up and down with every ragged breath.

"Dad?" I said.

I knelt down beside him. The ground was wet. I could feel it soaking through to my knees. I knew my trousers would get dirty, but I didn't care. I just wanted Dad to stop crying. I reached my arm around his shoulders.

"Why won't they come?" he said, in this sad voice that made my stomach freeze.

"What?" I said. "Why won't what come?"

"The words! They used to be so easy. I thought I had it. I thought this was how to get better. But it's not . . . it's not." His voice got quieter and quieter, until it was barely there at all. "My story," he muttered. I didn't know what to do, so

I squeezed him, I just squeezed him closer. "The words are gone, Owen. Just like she is. What do I do? What do I do?"

It was my fault. Half of Mum's paintings were wrecked. They littered the ground around us, and it wasn't Dad who did it, it was me. I was the one who'd stopped his writing. I was the one who'd made him like this. It was all my fault.

"I don't know," I said, feeling sick now.

"No," he said. "No. Neither do I." He picked up a fragment of painting. "But she would. She always knew what to do. And she's gone. She's gone . . ."

He was shaking again, crying silently into the wet mud.

*I don't know*, I'd said.

But it was a lie, wasn't it?

Because I did. I did know. I didn't want to go back into his story. I didn't want to live those pages. But I had to. I had to, because it was the only thing that could stop this.

Up in my room, I sent a text to Danny.

I've got to go again.

That was the truth. Even if it meant missing the academy trials altogether. I had to help Dad.

It wasn't long before my phone vibrated with Danny's reply. For a second, I hesitated. What if he was angry? He was upset when I missed the first game, but that was before he knew what was happening . . .

You can do it.

# 30

The next morning I was so concerned about making a plan that I forgot to prepare Dad breakfast like I normally did. When he slouched downstairs, he still had his bathrobe on, and he looked as if he hadn't slept all night. Dark splodges spread under his eyes, and his skin was paler than ever.

"Owen," he said, "about last night . . ."

"Don't worry about it."

"No, let me say it. I'm sorry. I really am. I had no right to do what I did. Those paintings, they're yours as well as mine. It wasn't right. I'm . . . I'm sorry."

"I'm sorry too," I said, and I really meant it.

"Come on, now. You've got nothing to apologize for."

I wished that were true, but it wasn't, was it? If it wasn't for me, Mum's paintings would all still be intact. They'd be hanging up just where she'd left them. Dad would still be writing and he wouldn't look like a sleepwalking zombie. It was all my fault.

And that meant it was up to me to make it better.


After roll call, I was the last one waiting in the classroom. Everyone else raced out as soon as the bell rang, but I couldn't go. Not yet. There was something I needed to do first.

I had to speak to Mrs. Willoughby. Tonight was the first parents' evening of the year. I was hoping that if I told her about Dad, she'd be able to help me. Maybe together we could get him to go back to his book.

"Is everything all right, Owen?" she said, peering up from her notes.

"Yeah," I said.

I'd practiced this over and over in my head. I crossed my fingers, just praying it worked. It *had* to. It had been ages since the last jump and I'd stopped fighting it ever since the game. If Dad wasn't writing, then I must have made him stuck by refusing to jump. I'd googled it last night, and found something called writer's block, this thing where you couldn't think what to write next. There were loads of people asking how to beat it, and the answers were things like:

- *Take a thirty-minute break and come back to it*
- *Go for a walk to clear your head*

- *Try writing a different story*
- *Just write through it*

If I was going to get back into the story, I needed to help Dad with number four.

"Um, Miss . . ." I said. I stood up, grabbing my bag. "You know this parents' evening thing tonight?"

"Mhmm."

"Would you be able to help me with something?"

"What do you mean?" she said.

"It's Dad. He's not . . . he's not coping very well at the moment. You know, with Mum and everything."

"Ah." Mrs. Willoughby looked up, making the Sad Face. But I didn't mind, because if she was listening then hopefully she'd want to help with the plan. "Right. Yes, I see."

"He's been writing this book. They said it would help."

"Who's 'they'?"

"His arts counselor. She thinks writing is a 'powerful window to the soul that can help heal wounds,'" I said.

"I see."

"And the thing is, you can tell it *does* help. The writing, I mean. When he's writing, his eyes light up, like there's this fire inside him. Which is good, because most of the time it's not there."

Mrs. Willoughby just listened.

"Anyway, he's stuck," I said. Now I'd started, I just wanted to get it over with. "I don't think he knows what to do. And I was thinking if someone asked him about the book, if they said it sounded good—you know—maybe it would . . ."

"Encourage him?" she said.

"Yeah. Yeah, something like that."

"You're a lovely boy, Owen. This shows real initiative, you know that?"

I didn't really know what she meant by that.

"Do you like the plan?" I said. "Can you help me?"

"Yes," she said, laughing abruptly. She turned away and in the reflection of the window she was wiping her eyes. "Yes, I can help you."

# 31

"I don't know," Dad said, later that evening. "Maybe I shouldn't go. I look like a zombie."

He was in the bathroom, shaving for the first time in days. He thought I was making it up when I told him about parents' evening, even though it was the millionth time I'd mentioned it. It was only when I dug out the letter that he believed me.

Now he was panicking and trying to get ready in a hurry, which always made bad things happen. He'd cut his skin or drop his toothbrush in the wastebasket again.

"You've got to go," I said. "Everyone else's parents will be there. If you don't go, then I can't go, and Mrs. Willoughby will mention it tomorrow and you'll make me look like an idiot in front of the whole class."

I waited outside the bathroom, messing around on my phone to take my mind off the plan. I was wearing my best T-shirt for good luck. It had a Superman design on it with a plane and bird's wings over the top, so at first you couldn't tell if was a bird or a plane or Superman.

I knew why Dad was nervous. It was because he hadn't been out of the house in ages. He'd been to the counselor, but that wasn't the same. It wasn't real-life stuff, like going to the store or going to the movies with friends or meeting a teacher at parents' evening.

Sometimes if I'd been injured and hadn't played football for ages, I got nervous about going back to training. It was worse if was a game. I got pre-game nerves so badly that it felt like a volcano erupting in my stomach.

I decided life was a lot like football. You had to get your uniform on and go out and give it your best shot. Dad was still in the locker room. He was still getting his uniform on, still fighting off the pre-game nerves.

"Anyway," I said. "Mrs. Willoughby wants to meet you. She said she's one of your biggest fans."

"Did she?" Dad said, over the buzz of the electric shaver.

"Yeah. She can't wait."

I knew it wasn't exactly the truth, but it wasn't the worst lie in the world, was it? I didn't know if Mrs. Willoughby *was* Dad's biggest fan, but if everything went well, she'd act like it. At least a bit. That was what I was hoping, anyway.

After a few minutes Dad emerged from the bathroom in a clean shirt and trousers, smelling of aftershave. It was loads better than the unwashed old clothes he usually wore around the house. He had bags under his eyes and his skin was still as white as chalk, but at least he was making the effort.

"Right," he said. "Let's get this over with, eh?"

The car park outside school was packed. Mums and dads and kids were filing out. The inky sky was crisp and clear and pinpricked with sparkling stars. I spotted Orion, hunting high above us, and thought about what I'd heard back in the story, about the stars being gods and heroes. I hoped it was a good omen, but I crossed my fingers for luck anyway.

"This way," I said to Dad, leading him through the tall glass doors. The receptionists had gone home, but there was a big board that said year 7 parents' evening and underneath it was an arrow pointing through a door to the big hall on the right.

I wished I could relax. The closer I got to the hall, the more nervous I became. My hands were sweaty, and I could feel my T-shirt sticking to my back.

*There's nothing to worry about.*

Mrs. Willoughby would help.

When we got to the door, I didn't know where to look first. All these tables were set out across the floor with teachers sitting behind them and kids coming or going or standing around talking to their parents. There was no space to move.

"Which one is your teacher?" Dad said.

I stood on tiptoes, squinting. At first I couldn't see her, then I caught something in the corner of my eye. She was waving from the far side of the room.

"There she is!"

When we got to the table, Mrs. Willoughby stood up and smiled at us. She shook Dad's hand and said it was lovely to meet him, and as we were sitting down she gave me a secret wink.

"I must say," she said, leaning in, "I've been looking forward to meeting you. I've only known Owen for a short while, but he's a very bright boy."

"He is," Dad said. My stomach was doing nervous backflips. So far, so good. "He takes after his . . . after his mother."

The last word dropped like a weight.

Silence.

*No.*

*This can't be happening*, I thought desperately.

I glanced at Mrs. Willoughby and made a face at her that said, *Do something!* because I could already feel the energy leaking out of Dad.

"Oh, but he must take after you as well," Mrs. Willoughby said. "I'm sorry—it's a little embarrassing to admit it to the parent of one of my pupils—but I'm a huge fan of your novel, Mr. Smith."

"You . . . you are?" Dad said.

"Oh, yes. *Time's Child* was one of my favorite books of the last decade. The underlying tones of hope and light, the accurate representation of social change . . ."

I didn't know what any of that meant. Maybe it was like the art thing, and Mrs. Willoughby knew how to find the hidden meaning. Or maybe she was just a brilliant actor, because whatever she was saying, Dad was lapping it up. He sat up straighter, leaning closer, nodding his head like one of those dogs you got for the backs of cars.

And then came the magic words.

"I can't wait for your next book," she said, staring him straight in the eyes. "What are you writing next?"

"Oh," Dad said. He paused. *Come on, Dad. Tell her!* "I'm wrestling with something at the moment, actually. It's inspired by quite a . . . dark time in my life. I wanted to write about fear and death and show how you can defeat it. But to be honest, I'm struggling a bit. I don't really know where to go next."

"Ah." Mrs. Willoughby smirked. "You're at *that* part of the book."

"What do you mean?" Dad said.

"Oh, one of my friends is an author. She got to the middle of her book and suddenly ran out of steam. She didn't know what happened next."

"And . . . and how did they get past it?" Dad said.

Mrs. Willoughby's eyes flicked to me, then focused back on Dad. "She just wrote," she said. "She wrote on the good days and then wrote on the bad days. Wrote even when it felt terrible. After that, she looked back and found that, actually, it was pretty good after all."

"Yes," Dad said. "Yes, perhaps."

"For what it's worth, I hope you do keep writing. It sounds brilliant."

"Er, thank you," Dad said, his cheeks reddening. "Thanks a lot."

Mrs. Willoughby opened her file. "Now I suppose we'd better get to this young man, eh? There's nothing to worry about, I assure you . . ."

I wasn't listening anymore. I was just trying to keep the grin off my face. My insides were jumping for joy, because it had worked. I *knew* it had worked.

A sudden shiver of fear crept in, interrupting my thoughts. I was going back to *Stormwalker*. I was going back to face the Darkness. And, if I was lucky, I was going to get through to Jack's dad.

# 32

I was ready for the swirling colors.

My head rang and my vision blurred, but I rubbed it away as the familiar fog filled my mind and Jack's thoughts trickled and mingled with my own.

Relief flooded through me, mingling with the sick feeling in my stomach.

I was back! It had worked!

Mrs. Cloud was going on about stars, but the words weren't sticking.

". . . they even drew patterns through the stars, to help envision them. You see the great Taurus, here? Of course, the night sky has been lost to us for years. It's impossible to say whether the stars themselves are real, or if they were simply part of the myth . . ."

A plan was forming in the back of my mind, but if it was going to work, I needed to find the plane. If anyone knew where the wreck was, it was him. I had to get to Quinn.

"Can I help you, Jack?" Mrs. Cloud said, as I stood up.

"I'll be back in a minute," I said. "Just . . . er . . . nipping to the bathroom."

I rushed out of the room and into the grayness of the day. The barrier of lights had been shut down. The Darkness was nowhere to be seen. The camp was so quiet. I guessed everyone was either out patrolling or in class.

*Where's Quinn?*

There! I spotted his truck. It was parked on the road, beside the half-destroyed Regent Street sign. I saw an LRP officer inside and ran over—

But it was James. His eyebrows knotted together as he looked up.

"I'm looking for Quinn," I panted. "Have you seen him? I—"

I stopped, because the look he gave me sent spiders scurrying over my back.

"Quinn's gone," he said.

"What do you mean? When's he getting back?"

"He's not. He left," James said. I blinked, shaking my head. I must have misheard him. Why would he leave? *How* could he leave? Unless . . . "Even LRP officers have to be held accountable," James added.

What did *that* mean?

I thought back to the last time I saw him—the panicked expression on his face.

I backed away, shaking my head. This couldn't be happening. I was imagining it, that was all. Maybe I wasn't in the story at all. Maybe I was just dreaming I was here.

I turned around and ran, glancing quickly over my shoulder. James was still watching me. I pumped my legs faster, working my way back to the cellar—

"Jack!" Iris said, crashing into me on the stairs. "Why did you leave like that?"

"Iris. Thank God. I was just asking James about Quinn and . . ."

I checked over my shoulder again, but the stairway was clear, at least for now.

"Yeah?" she said. "What did he say? Is he okay?"

Footsteps. Somewhere behind me.

I grabbed Iris by the hand and walked quickly into the hall, ducking into the shadows at the edge of the room.

"He said he's gone," I whispered.

"*Gone?* What do you mean 'gone'? They didn't take him to the Chamber, did they?"

"All I know is, Quinn knew about the plane. He made me promise not to check it out. Iris, he said something about the Marshal . . . he's been drugging you with lemon balm, to make you forget about things he doesn't want you to know. To make everyone forget."

"What?"

"Trust me, I'm telling the truth. I'll swear it on anything."

"The Marshal couldn't be drugging the whole camp," she said. "Someone would know about it. Someone would have seen."

"It's *true*," I told her, growing frustrated now. "Icarus 1 contacted us the other day, and he covered it up. But I think I've got a way to get back in touch with them."

"If the Marshal *is* drugging the camp, then how do *you* remember all this?"

"I . . . don't know," I said, though I thought I did. If there was something in the food, it might have affected Jack, but they couldn't do anything about me. "But I've got a plan. It involves the plane. I know," I said, holding up my hands to stop her protest, "you don't remember that, either. But I do. And if we can get the black box out of it, we might be able to use it to get through to Icarus 1."

Her eyes widened, and I looked round in time to see James striding through the cellar. Was he looking for me, or was I just being paranoid?

"Come on," Iris whispered. "We should get Farming, or we'll be *gone* too."

When it came to Hunting that afternoon, I didn't follow Seth's orders. Instead, I skirted around the edge of the camp, looking for anywhere they could have hidden the wreckage of the plane. On the edge of the north road, twenty yards away from the riverbank, an LRP officer was standing next to the door of a half-collapsed shop. He watched as we walked past, and I felt his gaze on me even as we rounded the corner and scanned along a nearby footpath.

"You don't have to help," I said to Iris, as we crept out of the way of a patrolling robot. "I'll just get you in trouble."

"How can I not help? Wouldn't be much of a friend then, would I? What are we looking for, anyway?"

"Just something out of the ordinary," I said. "Lumpy ground that wasn't there before. Anything that looks different or wrong. They couldn't have hidden it too far away."

We did two laps of the camp, exploring farther and farther into the wasteland, pretending to scavenge important items. But there was no hole in the ground, no cover-up.

It was as if the plane just disappeared.

"Maybe they dumped it out in the storm," I said. "If they did, who knows where it'll be. It could be anywhere. The Darkness might have turned it to dust."

I was just about to give up, when Iris stopped by the north road, twirling her slingshot between forefinger and thumb.

"What if we're looking for the wrong kind of weird?"

I followed her gaze. She was squinting over to the ruins of a nearby building. Behind them, the LRP officer was still standing by that same shop doorway.

"He hasn't moved for ages," she said.

Slowly, my brain clunked into gear and caught up.

If LRP's job was to patrol, to keep the camp safe, why would one of them be standing around like—

Like he was guarding something.

"I'll distract him," Iris said. "You take a look. I'll meet you in the cellar later."

And just like that, she ran off, scampering east through the rubble and skirting around the outside of camp.

I held my breath, wondering what to do.

I didn't want to risk going closer until she acted, but how would I know when to go?

Suddenly there was a shout. "Dreamless!" she cried, sprinting back through the ruins, kicking up swirls of dust.

The LRP officer looked up. He glanced around, seeming to weigh his options, then darted toward her. This was it. If I was going to move, I needed to do it now. I'd probably only have a few minutes, and if I got caught . . .

I crunched out of the shadows, tiptoeing through a canopied alleyway and out across the road. The door the man had been guarding was no different from any others in camp: blackened, like an old fireplace, the bricks all crumbling away.

But through the door—

I saw it right away. Charred and twisted metal. Smashed-up wings.

It was piled up in a corner at the back of the room, pieces strewn across the floor. And on its side, just visible in the shadows, faded black letters: icarus 1.

So it had been them! They must have been investigating after the radio call. I clambered over the wreckage, and dug my way through to what was left of the cockpit, careful not to slice my fingers on the broken glass.

*Where is it?* I thought. *It's got to be here, surely.* I tried to think back to that documentary I watched with Dad, the one about the plane crash, but I couldn't remember *where* the black box was kept. Panicking now, I reached farther into the foot space, feeling under the seat, and finally my fingers touched cold metal.

I gripped and tugged, and the box slid out. It was so big! There was no way I'd be able to get it out of there. Which bit was the location device? I held it up to the light. There were two main sections: a big square one, and a small cylinder. I pulled and twisted, but it wouldn't budge.

Footsteps, somewhere nearby, crunching on the gravel.

If I had to have guessed, I'd choose the cylinder over the box itself. I seemed to remember them mentioning that specifically on the show. I yanked harder. There was a sharp crack, and the cylinder snapped off.

I'd done it!

But I had to move . . .

Breathing quickly, I tucked the rest of the box back inside the cockpit. Then I dashed out, around the side of the building, and back toward the square.

"You were brilliant!" I said, when I found Iris in the cellar that evening. I didn't want to meet up with her right away, just in case anyone had seen us. If anyone found the location device, the whole plan would shatter just like that.

She smiled at me, and I beamed back, laughter bubbling up inside me. Someone had tried to hide the evidence of the plane, and the Marshal wanted us to forget about it—but we'd tracked it down. Now I just had to hope I could get the pinger to work.

When I was sure no one was looking, I held the cylinder out for Iris to see.

"What's it do?" she said.

"I . . . don't really know," I admitted. "Somehow it can be used to track crashed planes, though. I remember seeing a show on it once."

"You mean we went to all that trouble for nothing?"

"No," I said. "*They* went to all that trouble to hide it, which means it must be important. We just need to find a way to work it. I reckon it needs high ground, and daylight. It must be hard for it to work through the Darkness."

Her eyes flashed mischievously, the same way Danny's did back in the real world when we played games behind a teacher's back. "The radio tower. We go there so often that no one will suspect what you're doing. Except . . ."

"Except what?" I said.

"Well, you'll have to convince Seth. He's the one who tells us where to go, and the tower's quite far for a Hunting trip."

"Yeah," I said, suddenly nervous. "Yeah, you're right. But it's now or never. We've got to do it before the next Cleansing."

It wasn't going to be easy. We'd be out there without our illuminators. But I had to do something. Even though this was a story and that meant it was all in Dad's head and none of it was even real, it felt so much more than just words. It *was* so much more than just words.

Because I was right. I knew I was. I was here for a reason. I had to show everyone what the Marshal was doing. If Jack's dad was with Icarus 1, then I had to get to him.

I thought back to my real dad, smashing up all those paintings. If I could do this, maybe it would help. It had to help.

I kept the black box cylinder in my Hunting bag all through the next day. It might have been safe in the dorms, but I didn't want to risk it. Ever since Quinn's disappearance, I'd been checking and double-checking over my shoulder, just to make sure no one was watching.

After class, I walked quickly round the millet patch, avoiding the rough ground where the potatoes had just been planted, and only slowed down when I got toward the edge of the farm.

Seth was there again, running sprints.

He saw me when he turned back round, rubbing sweat from his forehead.

"What do you want?" he panted, jogging over.

I couldn't afford to mess this up. But now I was here, I couldn't think of the right words.

"I need to go to the tower," I said. "In the next daylight window."

Seth barked a quick laugh, then turned and ran again—short, sharp sprints, into the distance and back. When he swung back a third time, I tensed my legs, ready to run.

He spun and pelted off—and I bolted after him.

"What are you doing?" Seth growled, but his voice was snatched by the wind rushing past us.

I was beside him now, running parallel.

He skidded to a stop as I ran by, and leaned over, breathing heavily.

"Okay," he said. "You've got some pace, I'll give you that. But it's a long way to go. The illuminators won't be ready until this evening. What if you get caught out?"

"Just give me a chance. I . . . I've got an idea. I really think it'll work."

"We don't take ideas, Jack. We take orders. That's what we're trained for. That's why we're here. And we're under strict orders not to go too far in daylight windows, because you never know how long they're going to last. What's so important that it can't wait till later? Our priority's got to be contacting the City."

"What if I told you the City was dead?"

He stared at me. I held my breath, my heart pounding. It was a risk. I knew it was. But I had to get out there, and if that meant chancing a run-in with the Marshal again, then so be it.

Seth snorted. "I'd say you're going mad. Have you been to Cleansing lately?"

"No, and I'm not going back there anytime soon if I can help it. Seth, listen. None of this makes any sense. How long have we been here?"

"Six months. So what?"

"Think about it. No one could build a camp like this in six months. Not with the Darkness to contend with. The Marshal's lying to you, Seth. He's lying to all of us."

His mouth hung open, moving soundlessly. "What?" he said finally, shaking his head. "You're kidding, right? The Marshal's the only reason we're still alive."

"Look, if I'm wrong, you can chuck me out into the storm for all I care. But I've got a plan, and I know it can work. I just need you to get me to the radio tower. And . . . I need Iris with me. Send us in the direction of the tower when we go Hunting. Just this once. *Please.*"

I didn't dare break eye contact. I didn't want to give him any excuse to turn me down.

"Okay," he said, in this high voice that made it sound like even he couldn't believe what he was saying. "Just this once. But on one condition. I'm coming too."

# 33

I heard it before I saw it.

A marker pen squeaking, kids whispering, chairs rocking.

The world spun, turning upside down. I spread my arms to keep my balance, clenching my eyes tight shut, willing it to stop.

A burst of laughter rang out, and I opened my eyes.

I scanned the classroom for a familiar face, but these students . . . they weren't in my class.

They weren't even in my year.

The teacher narrowed his eyes at me. "Can I help you?" he said. One minute he would have been looking at his usual class, and the next I was there, staggering round like I was still half-asleep.

"S-sorry," I said, finding my way to the door. "Wrong class."

The corridor was empty. Everyone would be in a class.

I tried to remember where I'd been before, but everything was so vague.

*Deep breaths. Take it slow. I'm back. Everything's okay.*

I opened my timetable. I was supposed to be in English.

Walking slowly to avoid the groggy wave I knew was waiting to wash over me, I found my way to B corridor. Any second, I expected Mr. Barrow, the head teacher, to walk around the corner and bust me for being out of class.

I opened the door to the English class, trying to think of an excuse for being late. The whole class stared as I stood there in the doorway. I scanned the room and found Danny sitting at the back. He frowned at me, and I could almost see the cogs whirring in his brain.

"Sorry I'm late, Miss," I said. "I was in the nurse's office."

"Oh." Mrs. Cole paused by the whiteboard, pen in hand. "I could have sworn I marked you down as present," she said, the wrinkles on her face crumpling. "Or was it the other way around? Have . . . have you been in school all day?"

"Yeah," I said, as nonchalantly as possible.

"How strange," she said, staring at me for a long moment. Then she shook herself. "Okay, well, take a seat, Owen. We're just doing some more Shakespeare."

Normally I'd hate that sentence, but it felt so good to be called Owen again that I walked into the room feeling happier than I had in ages.

"There we go," Mrs. Cole said, noting the look on my face. "At least *one* of you is showing the excitement this text deserves!"

I took a seat next to Danny and slid my textbook out of the bag. It felt odd working at such a new-looking table, one that was clean and didn't creak like an old boat when you leaned on it.

"You were there, weren't you?" Danny whispered.

"Yeah," I said.

"Did it work? Did you find the plane?"

I nodded. "But I jumped back before I could take the black box to the hill."

"What about your dad? Is he all right?"

"I don't know. I guess I'll find out after school."


When I got home that afternoon, I walked slowly up to the front door. I waited there, not wanting to go in. I wasn't scared—just nervous. I kept picturing Dad smashing up those paintings, falling to his knees in the shed surrounded by all Mum's work. But he'd started writing again. He sent me back in. I just hoped that it hadn't all been for nothing.

I was standing at the door for so long that Dad saw me and came to let me in.

He smiled, and it wasn't just the half-smile, it was the nearly real smile. Relief flooded through me, and I couldn't stop beaming even if I'd wanted to. Because it was working! The plan was working.

"Forget your key?" Dad said.

"No. I was just thinking."

"About what?"

"Just stuff," I said.

I couldn't tell him that I was thinking about the story. About how I nearly messed up everything just because of football. Mr. Matthews is always saying we need to have a short-term memory. If you made a mistake, you forgot about it and moved on, and maybe you could do better next time. I had to put football well and truly out of my mind now.

"I've been writing again," Dad said, as he let me into the entrance hall. "I thought I'd be stuck forever, but the words are flowing."

"That's great!" I said. Then a sudden thought hit me. "Do . . . do you know how it's going to end?" I tried to look innocent, as if I didn't know anything about Jack or Iris or the Darkness.

Maybe if he told me more about the story, it would help me stay alive next time I jumped in. Maybe it would help *all* of us stay alive . . .

"No," he said. "To tell you the truth, I don't. I like finding out what happens while I'm writing. But I'll let you into a secret," he said, leaning closer. "I think there's a big death coming up."

My mouth dropped open.

A *death*?

My heart turned into a war drum beating louder and louder. I wished I'd never asked him. I wished I could invent a time machine just to go back and punch myself for thinking that question in the first place.

"Are you okay, Owen?" Dad said. "It's just a story."

Yeah, just a story. A story that I was living. A story where I could get hurt—where I could die. "I'm . . . I'm fine," I lied.

The writing may have been healing Dad, but right now it was the opposite for me. If I died in the story, what would happen to me here? Would I come back? Would I just stop existing? A tiny voice chirped up in the back of my mind, telling me not to jump. I could fight it again. I could force myself to stay here.

But I shut it down. I couldn't stop now. I'd come too far. And anyway, maybe I would be all right. It was Dad's story, but I was the one living it. I took a deep breath, trying to calm my nerves. I had the tracking device, and I had a plan. Seth had agreed to let me go to the tower. All I had to do was try not to die in the process.

# 34

Dazzling light—

Clamoring voices—

The world around me swirled into focus and I blinked back tears, trying to steady myself. Dad's words echoed in my mind again. *I think there's a big death coming up . . .*

Maybe it would be better if I didn't go out after all. *No.* I couldn't think like that. I had to finish the story. I was so close now. This was it: my chance to help Dad once and for all.

I felt the cylinder still tucked away in my pack. I just hoped getting to high ground would be enough for Icarus 1 to pick up the signal . . . they'd be able to locate us and send their airship. I'd reunite Jack with his dad.

Seth was waiting for us at the edge of camp, like always. Most of the Stormwalkers were there too, ready to make the most of the daylight pocket—however long it lasted.

"Okay," he said, when it looked like everyone had arrived. "The Darkness hasn't been playing nice lately. The Scholars don't think the light will last long. Try not to stay out longer than forty minutes. Listen for the siren. Keep your eyes and ears open, and stay safe."

He reeled off names, giving people directions to go in. Places where we might still find useful equipment, or locations where the Darkness had shifted the landscape and brought new bounty with it.

"Jack, Iris, Dillon," he said at last. "You're with me. We'll go toward the tower and see how far we get. Any sign of Darkness, we're coming straight back. I don't s'pose you're actually going to tell me the reason for all this?" he added in a low voice, when it was just us left.

"I don't want to jinx it," I said. "But you'll see."

With that, we ran off toward the radio tower, which loomed on the highest point of the horizon. The way we moved reminded me of how birds flew on long journeys. The bird at the back would fly to the front, taking the pressure off the leader. They kept cycling like that, so they could stay airborne for longer.

Seth ran in front, but after a minute whoever was at the back took his place. We passed long-dead glowroot meadows, no longer glimmering blue green, but plum colored and lifeless.

I didn't know how long we ran like that—scrambling over rocks and skidding down sweeping slopes, gradually getting closer to the hill with the tower on it—but every time we stopped for a breather my throat felt like sandpaper and my head pounded.

We pulled up beside one of the lamps we'd passed the first time I'd gone Stormwalking. In the Darkness, it would have flickered on automatically, but now it was off—as gray as the sky around us. Seth climbed a nearby rock, watching the horizon for any sign of the storm, but it was still quiet. The only sound was the noise the breeze made picking its way through the ruins, stirring up sand and dust.

A sudden flash of movement made me jump.

"What was tha—?"

Something smashed into me, sending me sprawling on the ground. Wheezing, I tried to stand up, but strong white hands were pinning me down.

With a hiss, the thing slashed at me. Its talons swiped within inches of my face. I cried out, but not because of how close it was.

Because I knew that face.

Seth slammed into the Dreamless, tumbling with it over the rocks. I scrambled to my feet, desperately gulping air into my burning lungs.

"Run!" Seth gasped, blocking a swipe with his forearm. "Get to the tower!" He collided with the Dreamless again, tumbling out of sight.

"It's him," I said, the words sounding dead on my tongue. Iris tried to drag me away, but I pulled free. "*It's him!*" My throat tightened. I couldn't breathe. Didn't they realize? He saved Iris on my first day in camp. He tried to help me. And now he was here, red-eyed and frothing at the mouth. "It's Quinn. They've . . . they've made him Dreamless."

Iris grabbed me again, and this time my legs jolted into life.

"Where's Seth?" I said. "We need to go back for him."

*Quinn* . . .

They'd done this because of me. It was all my fault.

"We need to get you to the tower," she yelled. She didn't let go of my arm. "It's like you said, it's now or never. Seth can look after himself. Come on," Iris muttered, "*move!*"

The ground sloped up, changing from lumpen road to jagged, rocky mounds. Tears stung my eyes, so I fumbled with my hands, gripping onto anything that could take my weight.

"It's not far," Iris said. Her face was strained, and white, so white.

Dillon didn't say anything at all, his face a determined mask.

And then we were up, and ahead of us now the flickering green glow of the power station pierced the dull gray of day. I was already digging in my pack, feeling for the cylinder. I held tight on to the cold metal and lifted it out, raising it as high as I could. I sprinted up to the building. The others rushed after me, bending over to catch their breath.

This was the highest point for as far as the eye could see. That was why they'd built the tower here in the first place. It *had* to work . . . it had to.

"What's that?" Dillon gasped. "What . . . what are you doing?"

This was what I was here for. This was what I had to do. Not just for me and Dad. For Iris, and Dillon, and Seth, wherever he was. For Quinn, so he hadn't been turned for nothing.

"We're supposed to be Hunting," Dillon said. "There's nothing here. We should keep moving."

"Just wait," Iris hissed.

She was looking up into the sky expectantly. Maybe I had to do something. A button I'd missed, or some switch. I held the cylinder up, examining it closely. But there was nothing.

"Come on . . ." I whispered.

I was so sure it would work. It had to. I thought it would be automatic, always on—a constant pinging radar. I thought if we could get it out of the Darkness, if we could get it up high, they'd be able to find us. This had been my idea. I'd brought them up here, away from the very things they were supposed to be finding.

A sudden screech rang out, gripping my heart.

No . . . no, not now.

I turned slowly, dreading what I was going to find. It was there on the horizon, just like the first time I jumped into this world. It rose up, painting the sky jet black. Then with one last sickening cry, it sped toward us.

# 35

"Darkness," Iris growled.

"We need to go," Dillon said. "I don't even know what we're doing here."

"He's right," Iris said. "It's okay, Jack. We can try again. We'll find a way. But we can't stay here."

"It's got to work," I muttered, holding the cylinder high again. I wished I'd paid more attention to the TV when that plane show had been on in the kitchen. I could remember everything about it—the crashes, the explosions, everything they'd said about the black box—except *how* it worked. I thought getting the device to high ground would activate it, but nothing was happening.

I'd . . . I'd failed . . .

"Let's go!" Iris cried. She grabbed a flashlight from her pack, holding it ready, and slid back down the uneven, sloping rocks. Shoving the cylinder into my pack, I rushed after her, drawing my own flashlight. But the ground was uneven and slippery. Clacking and tumbling, the stones gave way, and I skidded down the hill. My foot caught on a rock. I threw out a hand to stop myself falling, grazing my palm. Iris and Dillon helped me up.

"It's okay," I said. "We can make it."

But as soon as the words came out, I knew it was a lie. My legs were wobbly. The Darkness was getting too close. There was no way we'd be able to get back to camp, not before it reached us, and I wasn't sure how much protection three small flashlights could offer.

"The lamp!" Iris cried. "Quick!"

Heart racing, I sprinted in the direction she pointed, not daring to look back. I didn't need to know how close the storm was getting—I could hear it, hear it chittering, hear it whispering madly.

In the distance, the camp's siren wailed, letting everyone know of the danger. But we were hundreds of yards away, and the Darkness was too fast.

In the back of my mind, memories rose up—images of Mum in hospital with wires sticking into her skin and machines all around her . . .

*No—*

I smashed the image apart, refusing to let it take hold—

I couldn't afford to let the Darkness get to me. Not now.

I ran, the blood thundering in my ears, and flicked the flashlight on, sending its beam stabbing back over my shoulder. The storm cried out in protest as Iris and Dillon did the same. *Come on*, I said to myself, willing my legs to move faster, *come on . . .*

And then we reached the lamp. It clicked on and a high-pitched shriek split the air again as the clouds whipped away, swirling out of reach. The Darkness surrounded us, leering angrily, but for the time being at least we had our own bubble of protective light.

I put my hands behind my head to open up my lungs, and breathed deeply. It was only a short sprint. It couldn't have lasted very long at all, but it felt like forever. Dillon hunched over as if he was going to throw up. Iris turned toward me, breathing heavily, her cheeks flushed red.

"Are you okay?" she said.

"Yeah," I panted. I looked around at the blanket of impenetrable black. Menacing lights flickered wherever I looked, in the shape of faces. "What are we going to do now?"

There was nowhere to go—nowhere that didn't involve fighting right *through* the storm.

Then I remembered what Dad said before I jumped. An idea came to me, surprising me by how ready I was to try it. I thought I would be more scared, but I wasn't, not now. I might have failed at communicating with Icarus 1, but maybe there was still something I could do to help. They said the Darkness fed on fear, didn't they? That was why it dragged those memories out of me. That was why I could hear Mum's voice whenever it got close. Well, I'd seen some scary things in my time. Things no kid should ever see.

"You need to find Seth," I said, dropping the flashlight on the ground. "Make sure he's okay."

"What do you mean, *you*?" Dillon said. "And why are you dropping your flashlight? You're coming with us."

The storm reached out an inquisitive tendril, which sizzled in the light from the lamp and pulled back. Fresh screeches rang out, splitting the sky.

"Grab Iris and get ready to go," I said, unclipping my Hunter's pack. It was so much easier to breathe with the clasps open. Yes . . . Maybe this was why I was here. I'd give it fear. I'd give it more fear than it had ever had in its life.

"What are you doing?" Iris demanded, rounding on me.

"I've got a plan," I said. It was so much effort trying to talk over the storm. I didn't tell her that all I could think to do was to try something stupid and hope for the best. Maybe it could buy them some time to get to the next light, to get back to camp, instead of following my crazy idea.

"Jack—"

"Get ready to go!" I shouted, summoning all the strength I could. "I'll distract it. You said it feeds on our fears—well, I hope it's hungry."

"Jack, no!" Iris cried. "I won't let you!"

All I knew was there was something inside me and for all this time I'd ignored it. Because it was so much easier to pretend it wasn't there. But I couldn't pretend anymore.

"Jack!"

Dillon grabbed Iris and dragged her away, right to the edge of the bubble. Iris struggled against his grip, desperate to break free, to come back for me.

I counted to three, then threw my Hunter pack into the Darkness. It disappeared from view, then landed with a splash in the river. There were two location devices in a black box, weren't there? One for the ground, and one for the sea. I couldn't figure out how to work the first one, but with a bit of luck, the river would activate the second.

"Come on then," I said, glaring up at the storm. I wasn't scared of becoming Dreamless now. Maybe I was never meant to find Jack's dad. But I could buy the others some time, at least. Help them get back to safety after I stupidly lured them into the storm with me. Not all characters could live happily ever after, could they?

"JACK!" Iris cried, as I stepped back, out of the light, and into the raging Darkness.


I knew what memory it would be. I knew what the storm wanted me to see.

*I'm standing outside the hospital ward. Dad's holding Mum in his arms. They don't know I'm here. They think I've gone to buy them drinks.*

*Even though Mum's been in pain for months, she's never cried.*

*But when I left the room, she must have given in.*

*She must have broken down.*

*Because now she's not fighting, she's not holding it off. The tears are flowing out of her eyes and trickling down her face.*

"Yes," I croaked, as the Darkness whipped and snapped around me . . .

Because it was working—the plan was working. The dark clouds snapped at the air, lashing out. I did my best to ignore them. Because this was it. This was the moment. My mind filled with images of Mum, of Dad beside her.

*The machines around Mum are beeping, the nurses rushing me out—*

*I'm looking at her through the window, seeing her white face, her sunken eyes—*

*Now we're back at home and she's in bed, gagging and retching—*

Pain racked my body. I wanted to give in. I wanted to let go. Being Dreamless would be better than this. Anything would be better than this.

*No.* Not yet.

I shook my head, making my voice louder.

"You're going to have to do better than that," I shouted.

I held Mum in my arms. I saw her eyes fade. All this time I'd called it the Longest Day because all she could do was lie in bed and all we could do was watch. But Mum died before the Longest Day—she died as soon as she got that stupid leukemia.

There . . .

"I could never say it before," I said, the words thick in my throat. "But I can say it now. Leukemia! *Leukemia, leukemia, leukemia!*"

My eyes burned with the tears streaming down my cheeks. I opened myself up—letting all the memories flood out. My body sagged as the energy drained out of it and I fell onto the hard ground. I wanted to get up, to have one last look at Iris and Dillon. I wanted to see if they'd made it to safety. My arms wobbled, straining with the effort. Then I collapsed.

The Darkness loomed over me and I knew that this was it.

Dad was right. There *was* a death coming.

This was the end.

# 36

Nothing.

Nothing in every direction. I tried to get up, but my arms were too cold, my legs too heavy. I couldn't move. Panic screamed through me—

And I realized something else. Something far scarier than my numb body.

I wasn't breathing. I opened my mouth, but my throat was so dry that no sound came out. What was happening to me?

*Drink.*

The thought flickered out of nowhere, but now that it was there, I couldn't shake it. It was more than a thought. It was a need.

*Drink.* I needed water.

Grimacing with the effort, I rolled onto my side. Everything was white. A never-ending sea of white, and a quiet so loud that my ears rang with it.

I cleared my throat. "Hello," I said, testing the word. It came out more like a croak.

"Hello?" I said, louder now. There was no reply. *Am I dead?* I thought. *Is that what this is?*

*The Darkness*, I thought with a sudden pang. It had been so close to Iris and Dillon. They were in danger because of me. I was supposed to get through to Icarus 1. I was supposed to reach Jack's dad. But I'd failed.

"Iris!" I shouted, trying to sit up again. "Dillon!"

"They're not here," said a voice.

I froze.

Hearing Iris wouldn't have surprised me. Any of the people from Dad's story, I could have coped with. But that wasn't Iris or Quinn or any of the others.

That was—

That was Mum.

The shock jolted my muscles awake. I scrambled back, but it was impossible to tell if I was going anywhere. There was nothing to judge my movement by.

It couldn't be Mum.

This was just another memory. The Darkness was still feeding, it had to be.

"Where are you?" I called. Maybe this was what happened when you became Dreamless. Maybe everything got taken away until this was all that was left.

"Somewhere in your father's head," Mum's voice said. "This is where all his characters go, when their time is up."

"W-what? What are you talking about?"

There was movement at the other end of the room.

*Room? Is that what this is? A room?*

As soon as I thought it, the whiteness shifted. Shapes formed in it, and out of nowhere some walls appeared. They were still white, but not as bright. An off-white. A hospital white.

Now there was a bed in the corner of the room, with machinery around it. Wires and coils, and a horrible humming noise.

"Oh no," Mum said. "I'd rather not go back there. Can't you make it something else? Something nice?"

"What do you mean? I don't understand."

"You don't have to understand," she said. "You just have to think, and feel. You'll see. Try it now. Don't think about the bad days. Think about the good ones."

There was a crack in the wall. I peered through it.

There was Mum pushing me on the swings. There was Dad taking me to my first football game. Now we were sitting in the park, the three of us, having a picnic and enjoying the sunshine.

"Yes," Mum said. "That's better. That'll do."

"How are you here?" I asked. "You *died*."

"Yes," she said. "I did. But you don't have to be alive to be a character in someone's story."

"Am . . . am I dead too?"

"Yes," she said. "And no."

"What do you mean?"

"It's up to you. After all, it's your story, just as much as your father's."

The cold feeling drained away. I spun round, looking for Mum in the nothingness, but her voice was gone now.

"Mum!" I called. "Mum, come back!"

Orange flickered at the edge of my senses—

And everything broke apart.

# 37

Screaming. Constant, high-pitched screaming.

The orange light flared and flickered. Fire. It was all around me.

"Thought I'd lost you there," yelled a voice, and as the fog cleared, I realized it was Seth.

"You're okay," I spluttered through cracked lips. I shook my head, trying to gather my senses. What on earth had just happened? Mum . . . she had been so real.

I reached out and Seth gripped my arm, hauling me to my feet. My knees gave out under the weight, but he held me steady. With his spare hand, he swirled the stick of fire around us.

We were still outside camp, still in the wasteland, but the Darkness wasn't even trying to get close. On the horizon it raged as strong as ever, but here . . . it had retreated high into the sky.

"What . . . what's going on?"

"A very good question," he said, and for a second I was sure I saw a smile on his lips. "But I was hoping you'd be able to tell me the answer to that. You're the one who did it."

The Darkness was higher than I'd ever seen it. It was like we had an invisible wall above us, stopping it getting closer. In the distance, I could make out Iris and Dillon waving from beside a glowroot meadow. They'd managed to get away. They hadn't been hurt.

My fear . . . there was so much of it before, but now there was something else where the fear used to be. Before now, I couldn't handle the bad memories. There were too many of them. But now they were gone. Maybe the Darkness couldn't handle them either.

For a second I felt elated. I'd bought Iris and Dillon time. They'd made it to safety. Then I remembered the black box, and my stomach plummeted.

"My idea didn't work," I said, as the memory of the hill came crashing back. Even chucking the location device in the water didn't seem to have lured Icarus 1 here. "I'm sorry."

"You can apologize later," Seth said. "Let's get back to camp first."

He helped me over the rough ground, and we worked our way toward the meadow where Iris and Dillon were standing. Seth ditched the stick before we got too close to the plants.

Iris marched over to me and smacked me on the shoulder. "What was that about?" she shouted. "You could have got yourself killed!"

"I don't know what you did," Dillon said, his face pale even in the dark, "but it was brilliant. The Darkness just sort of . . . ran away."

I looked up at the storm again. It was still there, seething, but it wasn't coming any closer. "I don't know what I did either," I said, which was pretty much the truth. The back of my neck tingled as I thought about that place I went to—its shifting walls, the sheer whiteness.

And Mum . . .

"Come on," Seth said. "They'll probably be waiting for us."

We set off back toward camp. My legs burned as if I'd run a marathon, and I still had the remains of a stitch in my side. My skin prickled where the Darkness had got so close. But we were okay—somehow, all of us had made it.

When I saw the LRP officers lining the edge of the light barrier, I thought they were going to cheer us on. The rest of camp was standing behind them, the timetable forgotten. But they didn't clap or cry out. They just stood there.

As soon as we made it through the light, they grabbed us.

"You're coming with us," they said, "at the express order of the Marshal."

*What?*

I tried to fight free, but the grip on my arms was too tight. "Where are we going?" I demanded, kicking up dust as I struggled to match their pace. "Where are you taking us?"

And then I saw.

They marched us through the square, up to the church, where the Marshal had argued with Quinn. Through the curtains they dragged us, and into the building itself. The Marshal was sitting there in his high-backed chair, waiting.

When he saw us, he clapped—loud, echoing in the open space.

"Bravo. A solid effort indeed," he said, a mad glint in his eyes. "You can chuck your Hunter gear over there. You won't be needing the packs anymore. Your time in this camp is at an end."

Seth was breathing heavily, his shoulders rising up and down like a lion. Iris and Dillon huddled together, the same shock I was feeling plastered all over their faces.

After all that, it had all been for nothing?

"You don't deserve to make that decision," I spat, sounding loads braver than I felt.

"Oh? And why is that?"

"Tell them," I said. "Tell them what you've been hiding from them."

"You *are* a clever one," the Marshal said, his eyes narrowing to sharp points. "Tell me . . . how do you know? No one knows. No one remembers. *No one!*"

"I never did like drugs," I said.

"Hmm. Shame. Well, no drink for you, then. As for you three—" he clicked his fingers, and an LRP officer brought in a tray of drinks; I could smell the lemon balm drifting off them from here—"you can have a choice. But first, I'll tell you a little story. Leave us," he added to the LRP officers, before folding his hands on the table, and staring at Iris, Dillon, and Seth in turn.

"The City is dead," he said. Seth and Dillon gasped. Iris just stood there glaring back at the Marshal. "We found it after our first year at camp. After so long without hearing from them, Quinn suggested we go looking. We didn't have the airship, so we had to drive. It took three cars to make it to the walls, and over a week to finish the trip. But . . ."

He stopped to clear his throat.

"We were too late. There was nothing left. Nothing but bones and dust. The buildings of London ruined. Buckingham Palace, crumbled and deserted. The dome of St. Paul's Cathedral crushed. The streets littered with rubble, all the buildings overgrown with ivy. It wasn't pretty."

This wasn't right. It wasn't supposed to end this way. I was supposed to finish the story and get home, back to the real world, with school and Danny and football and Dad all better.

But Dillon spoke first. "No," he said.

"No what?" said the Marshal.

"I don't believe you."

"It is not a case of whether you believe it or not, boy. This world is dead. We are the last survivors. You should be thanking me! Think of all I have given you. Would you rather live out your days in despair, or enjoy at least an illusion of hope? At least you *thought* you could do something. At least you *thought* you were heroes. Better that than sitting around, waiting to die. You can go right back to feeling like that now, if you want. All you have to do is drink."

He indicated the three glasses, before him on the table. Somehow, he must have found a way to work his lemon balm medicine into the liquid.

"Don't drink it!" I yelled. "Don't drink it. You'll just go round and round like this forever."

I thought of Dad, back home, never able to throw Mum's ashes out to sea. And me . . . I was just the same, wasn't I? Hiding from the Longest Day. Hiding from Mum's leukemia.

"You can't hide from the truth," I said. "All it ever does is make things worse."

"Drink," the Marshal cooed. "Drink it, and you can leave. Drink it, and all this will be gone. You can live a life full of hope once more."

"You're a liar," I spat. Something had flickered inside me when the cylinder hadn't worked. It burned hotter and hotter, fueled by the anger and the frustration. It had been replaced by the cold certainty that I was going to die as the storm closed in. But now that I was still here, I was determined to put up a fight. "Tell them. Tell them what you've been hiding."

The Marshal's eyes reduced to sharp points. His nostrils flared, but when he spoke, his voice was calm and measured. "You really do remember, don't you?"

"I remember all of it. How you turned Quinn Dreamless. How you covered up the plane, just so no one found out about Icarus 1. How you hid the radio call from the whole camp . . ."

"Hmm. Well, it was a shame to have to exile Quinn. He was tremendously useful. Took a great deal of persuading to follow my plan too. He was desperate to get through to the City. I, on the other hand, couldn't allow us to reunite with them. It was easy enough to influence the memories of such a small camp, but the whole City? No, no, no. Far better to stay hidden. Isolated. Free from their filthy ideals.

"I don't expect you to understand. How could you? You're a boy, a duplicate. You couldn't possibly understand the stresses of managing so many lives. I wasn't supposed to be here at all, you know. I would much rather have been back in the City. I had a plan, a perfect plan, to cull the population, but Quinn, your father and the other Marshals put a stop to it. If they'd let me have my way, maybe the City would still be alive. But now look at me. I'm here! And they are not."

"Quinn?" Iris said. "What do you mean, Quinn and the other Marshals?"

"He was a Marshal, back in the City. He was supposed to lead Icarus 3. How different things would have been, eh? If little old me hadn't snuck aboard and crashed the ship. I couldn't exactly stay, could I? Not after my plans had been exposed. He tried to fight me at first, but everyone has a weakness, if you're clever enough to find it. He was very fond of you," he added, glaring at me. "After I forced his best friend onto Icarus 1, all I had to do was *hint* at your untimely demise, and he would do whatever I asked of him."

"The other camps will stop you," I said. He was sounding more and more mad with every second, but I couldn't think of anything to do apart from talk. "They'll put an end to all this."

"Ah, yes, the others," he said. "You're quite right, they'll certainly try. If they can find us."

Dillon was staring at the Marshal, his mouth hanging open. He tried to interrupt him, but all that came out was a strangled squeak.

"What is it, boy? Speak up."

"You . . . you said we'd never heard from them. You said they must be dead."

"Of course I did. I couldn't have anyone interfering, could I? We picked up their frequency within weeks. Icarus 2 was transmitting a distress signal. It ended soon enough, as, I'm sure, did they. Shame. As for Icarus 1, they were most persistent. At first I thought they wanted to steal our glory, but after we found the City dead, I realized they wanted more than that: they wanted to steal our land. So I thwarted their efforts to communicate. With Quinn's help, I kept us isolated, and thanks to my medicine, no one suspected a thing. Until *you*," he said, glaring at me again.

"I heard the radio call from Icarus 1," I told him. "They said something about Operation Phoenix. That doesn't sound like they want to steal our land. It sounds like they want to team up."

"It's the same thing," the Marshal spat. "I didn't know how close they were to finding us until that plane crash. Your father will want to dispose of me, I'm sure, but he'll never locate our camp."

"You're insane!" I said, my mind racing. I looked quickly around for something, anything that could help, but there was no way out. All I could think to do was keep him talking, keep Iris and the others from drinking that lemon balm.

"Very likely, yes," the Marshal said, the ghost of a grin playing on his thin lips. "Only a madman would have left the City on one of these Icarus projects in the first place."

I chanced a glance at the others. All this time they'd been thinking they were saving their families, but they were all gone. It had all been for nothing. I knew how much they wanted to forget it. Until today that was what I'd have done too. But I had to stop them. I had to do something...

The Marshal stood up and stalked back and forth behind the table. "Now, enough talking. The time has come for you to choose your fate. It will be a shame to get rid of such good Stormwalkers, but everyone is disposable if they are a threat to my camp."

He advanced on us, eyes flashing.

"Do it. Take the drink, or join your friend Quinn. One little sip is all it takes . . ."

I glanced nervously at Iris. Her eyes were wet. She'd watched her parents become Dreamless, and now she knew her brother and auntie were both dead too. Dillon, Seth—they both had family in the City as well. One little slurp, and it would all be gone.

"I've got the black box," I said quickly.

I knew it was a lie. The cylinder was floating somewhere in the river. But maybe the shock of it would buy us more time.

The Marshal's mouth opened in surprise, but he quickly covered it up. "No matter," he said. "The radio transmitter is useless in the Darkness. The only way it could work is if—"

He stopped, mouth working silently.

"Is if—" he said again, but still the words didn't come out.

And then I realized why.

Because somewhere high above us, there came a deep rumbling sound.

The *thrum-thrum-thrum-thrum-thrum* of airship propellers.

# 38

I rushed outside, Iris and Seth and Dillon on my heels.

I hardly dared believe it. The location device . . . it must have clicked on when it hit the water. It worked! It actually worked! High above us, blinding lights blasted their way through the storm, then merged with the light from camp.

"Clear the landing zone," a strong female voice boomed, echoing through loudspeakers.

I staggered back as dust whipped up in the swirling wind. Up close, the propellers were so loud you couldn't even hear the Darkness.

The top of the airship looked like a helicopter with rotor blades whirring round and round, but the bottom was a kind of balloon boat, with two great legs on either side to land securely. Across the side, stenciled letters read: ICARUS 1—NEW LONDON.

"No!" cried the Marshal, behind us. "No—what are you doing?"

"Marshal Davenport," crackled the voice through the speaker, "you are under arrest. Remain where you are and do not resist."

A ramp lowered, thudding at our feet. A squad of LRP officers hustled down to detain the Marshal before he could run away. He cried out, punching and flailing, trying to fight his way free.

"I insist you let me go," he spat. "Let me go this instant!"

They dragged him onto the ship. A woman appeared on the ramp, a leather jacket over her dress, and a pair of dusty-looking aviator goggles strapped to her forehead. Another group of LRP officers followed her down and started speaking to the rest of our camp, explaining what was happening and helping them on board the ship.

"We've been looking for you for a long time. I'm Vanessa," she said. "Mayor of New London. How would you like to see the City?"

"The C-City?" I stammered. "I . . . I thought the City was destroyed?"

Had the Marshal been lying to us again?

"Oh, it was," Vanessa said. Her smile faltered. "We only managed three rescue trips before the eastern lights failed. The people rioted, trying to get on board. As soon as one light smashed, the Darkness found a way in. By the time we got back for the fourth group of evacuees, it was a wasteland. But we're building a new one," she said, tapping the hull of the ship proudly. "New London. We found out your camp was alive when we saw the security footage of Marshal Davenport discovering the City ruins. He was never supposed to be on board Icarus 3, so we knew he had to be up to something sinister."

Suddenly I stopped walking along the deck of the ship. I squinted into the distance, something flickering in the back of my mind. Jack's thoughts exploded and danced.

"Vanessa," I said. "The people you rescued—the ones from the City . . ."

"Families of the Icarus crews had priority boarding," she said, the smile returning to her face now. "Follow me. There are some people who have been dying to see you. It was impossible to turn them away when we saw the sonar."

Footsteps thudded on the wooden decking. An explosion of voices rang out.

"Iris!" someone called. "Iris, over here!"

"Seth, buddy!"

A crowd of people ran toward us. I knew they were the mums and dads, the brothers and sisters of everyone in our camp. I watched Dillon work his way tentatively across the railing, looking for his family. When they saw him, his parents rushed over and dragged him into a giant bear hug. I laughed, an odd mixture of feelings wrapping round each other inside me. We'd done it. We'd beaten the Darkness. We'd beaten the Marshal.

"Jack!" a voice called, and I recognized it at once.

It was the same one I'd heard days earlier, on the radio.

"Jack, my son!"

Jack's dad skidded on the wooden planks in his haste to make it over to me. His brother, Ayden, was right behind him. I ran toward them, happiness soaring inside me. I let my thoughts, the ones belonging to plain old Owen Smith, retreat back into the fog. This was Jack's moment.

We collided, all three of us, hugging each other tight.

"You're alive," they said. "Oh, I can't believe it. You're alive!"

As the airship wobbled up and up and up into the air, I pulled myself away from Jack's family and saw Iris. I held my little fingers to the corners of my lips and let out a long whistle. She looked up, her cheeks shining, and ran over to me, hugging me just as tightly as Jack's dad had.

"We did it," I said.

"*You* did it," she said. "If it wasn't for you, we'd still be back there." She pulled away, her eyes still wet with tears. "Seriously, thanks . . . *Owen*," she added, so only I could hear.

I looked around at Seth, Iris, and Dillon, and the family Jack would be living with as they built New London together. I couldn't believe how lucky he was to have them all here.

Any second now I'd feel the tug, and there wouldn't be any more story. It would just be me and Dad. But he needed me. And, I realized, as we flew higher and higher and the story started to break apart at the edges, I needed him too.

# 39

My heart refused to calm down. It felt like it was trying to break out of my chest. I didn't dare to move, and waited, holding my breath. What if it hadn't worked? What if I was just in a dreamed-up version of home? What if there was no way back?

I let my eyes open.

Curtains. They looked like my curtains.

And the bed . . . that was mine too. There was the chip from when I practiced free kicks. Footballers stared down at me from the walls.

There was a glass of water on the windowsill. I didn't know how long it had been there—it must have been days at least—but I grabbed it and gulped it down.

My stomach cramped with hunger and my T-shirt was drenched in sweat.

How long had I been away? I fumbled for my phone, and slid it open. December 13. I couldn't remember the last time I was here. It was all blending together. No beginning or end, just one long stream of jumps.

I sent a quick text to Danny:

Are you there, mate?
Yeah. What's up?

I fell back onto the bed, beaming. Laughter erupted out of me and I couldn't stop it. *I did it. I finished the story.*

I closed my eyes and listened to the silence. I wanted to just *be*. To melt into the bed and not think about anything. But I needed to see Dad.

I had to know for sure that I'd helped him.

Feeling like a zombie, I finally rolled out of bed. I put on some sweatpants and a sweater and headed out onto the landing.

His bedroom door was ajar. The light was on. But when I peeked through the crack, the room was empty.

Taking a deep breath, I walked downstairs, using the banister for support. Treading carefully, I made my way toward the study.

Dad was sitting at his desk.

I took one deep, slow breath to calm myself down. In through my nose and out through my mouth, just like Mr. Matthews taught us when we were running sprints at training.

"Dad?" I said, standing in the doorway, not daring to go in.

Paper was strewn all over the floor. Torn and scrunched-up pages, scattered files and folders.

"Are you all right?" I asked.

He turned, and his face was lined and gray. There were bags under his eyes. It looked like he hadn't shaved for days.

"I think I've done it," he said. "I think I've finished the book." A smile crept across his face. His eyes shone, and color returned to his cheeks. He looked happy, for the first time in such a long time.

"Nice one," I said, grinning right back.

Dad waved his hand, beckoning me to come in. He shifted up so I could sit next to him.

"Here," he said. "Look."

The book was on the desk in front of him. Jack, the storm, the Darkness: it was all there on the first page, and I didn't need to see the rest to know what happened.

"It felt so good, Owen," Dad said. "It felt so good to write. Everything just sort of . . . clicked."

I pictured all the jumps—all the things I went through. All those people. Iris and Quinn and the others. They all felt real. They *were* real, for as long as I was there.

I wondered what they were doing now. Would they go to the place where Mum was? Or would they be making a new life in New London?

Happiness drifted off Dad in waves. He smiled a proper smile again and it felt like balloons were swelling up inside my stomach because, *Look at him!* His face crinkled in places I'd forgotten it crinkled. He shook his head. He beamed, and even though we were sitting in silence I could have sat there for hours and never got bored.

The next day, we both went out to Mum's art shed.

We were surrounded by her paintings. What was left of them, anyway.

Before, when I asked Dad what he most loved about Mum, he couldn't answer. He just got angry. But now the words rushed out. I learned things about her that I never knew. He told me all about how she got offered a job in New York but turned it down because it was just before I was born and she wanted me to live in England.

That was the thing about parents, wasn't it?

They did mum and dad things and you got on with doing *your* own thing, like playing football or playing on the PlayStation. You didn't ask them questions. Not real questions. Like when had you had your first boyfriend or girlfriend, or when had you been more scared than you'd ever been in your life, or what was the most disgusting thing you'd ever eaten?

So there was all this stuff that was there, and you just didn't know it.

"What's the first memory you have of her?" I asked Dad.

"Ah," he said. He looked up at the ceiling, as if it was all playing out again from a TV above him. "It was the summer ball, at university. She was wearing a red dress, and she . . . she was so beautiful. It was the first time I'd ever seen her. I knew then I had to be with her. My turn," he said, clearing his throat. "What was the funniest thing she ever did?"

"That's easy," I said. "We'd just come back from school, and I ran on ahead. But Mum had the house keys. She tried to chuck them to me across the drive. She wound her arm up, swinging it round and round like a cartoon character. But when she let go, the keys flew backward. They landed right in the middle of the road and got run over by a car."

"So *that's* why the key's wonky," Dad said, chuckling to himself.

The more we talked, the more real Mum felt. She wasn't distant and faded anymore. She was back in full color.

After a while, we walked out to the car, and sat in silence while the windows demisted. I held the urn in my hands, just thinking about Mum. All the old memories, but the new ones too.

Dad reversed out of the drive, and we set off for Brighton. After all the failed attempts at making the trip, I thought it would feel odd when we finally left the house.

But there was nothing strange about it.

It took almost three hours to get there, but it passed so fast because all we were doing was talking about Mum. When we arrived, Dad parked near the promenade and led the way to the pier.

"This is where we had our first date," he said.

I'd always imagined what it might look like. I'd pictured a few wooden planks, with not much around it. But it wasn't like that at all. There were bright lights everywhere, and the sound of music and laughter carrying on the air. It wasn't just a pier—it was a fairground on the sea.

I passed the urn to Dad, and together we walked along the pier. As soon as we set foot on it, the wind picked up. Seagulls soared overhead, screeching and crying out.

We weaved between the crowds, dodging people's photos and overexcited kids. The smell of fish and chips mingled with popcorn and doughnuts and cotton candy, making my stomach rumble.

It took ages to get to the end. There were more rides there, but if you stood right by the fence and looked out over the sea, there was finally a bit of quiet.

From up here, the water looked like it stretched on forever—choppy waves and streaks of white slicing across the gray and blue.

"Well," Dad said. "Here we are."

He looked down at the urn. Mum's ashes had been in our house for so long, sitting on the mantelpiece. But they wouldn't sit there anymore. They'd drift out in the water, with the fish and the crabs and all the odd-looking creatures that lived on the sand.

Dad sighed, and turned to look back. "This is where we first kissed," he said. "With the sea behind us, and the fairy lights overhead."

I moved closer to Dad and put my arm around him. He took a deep breath, and I squeezed him to let him know that I was here with him, that I wasn't going anywhere.

"Are you ready?" he said.

"Yeah. I'm ready."

The wind picked up again, whistling around us. Dad took one last look at the golden urn, then he flung the ashes over the railing. They hung in the air for a moment, picked out in the red and green lights and the last of the afternoon sun, and then they dropped silently into the cold, gray water.

# 40

When the academy trials came round, Dad was there in the crowd.

We were at the team training ground, which was a park a million times better than any I'd ever played on before. Dad's voice rang out every time I made a tackle, and when I scored my first goal the ref had to give him a warning for running onto the pitch.

"Nice one, Owen!" he yelled. "Get in!"

After the game, as the parents walked back to the car park and the players filtered into the changing rooms, I stayed out on the pitch, taking it all in. The grass had been perfect at the start of the game, but it was ripped and torn now, with deep slashes where studs had shredded the mud.

"Are you all right?" said Danny, jogging over.

"I'm fine," I said. "I'll catch up with you in a sec."

"Okay," he said. He lingered for a second more, then turned and followed the guys away.

I listened to the low rustle of the wind in the trees, and the quiet tweeting of the birds. I looked up at the sky, clear and blue, dotted with low white clouds. I imagined what it would look like with a storm of Darkness raging above it.

Wherever Iris was now, I hoped she was safe.

I hoped she was happy. I hoped all of them were.

Taking a deep breath, I raised my little fingers to my mouth, and let out a long whistle.

The birds went quiet. For a moment, the trees stopped rustling. Then a lone bird chirped up, and the others joined in, and all the sounds of the day came flooding back.

I picked up my bag and threw it over my shoulder, heading toward the changing rooms.

# MEET MIKE REVELL!

I've always enjoyed writing stories, but it wasn't until I read *Harry Potter* that I knew I wanted to be an author.

I was one of those kids who just didn't like reading. There were some books I liked, like *The Hobbit* and anything by Roald Dahl, but I would much rather run home and play on my PlayStation than dive into a book. They just seemed so boring. They took too much time to get into.

Then *Harry Potter* came along, and it changed everything.

I devoured the first, second, and third books in quick succession. It wasn't just enjoyable reading them—it was thrilling. I grew up with Harry and will always remember the painstaking wait for the postman to come to the door with the newest book, and the sheer joy at diving in and losing myself in the story for the rest of the day.

Reading those stories made me realize just how wonderful books could be. That's why I wanted to be a writer—to try and give people the feeling that I had all those years ago, when I suddenly thought . . . wow.

Now, I love telling stories about old things, like myths or fables, in new ways. My first book, *Stonebird*, is based around the idea of gargoyles coming alive in the silver glow of the moon. It's also quite heavily influenced by real life. After seeing my grandma suffer from dementia for a number of years, I wanted to write about the importance of memories and the magic of stories.

**Want to know more about Mike?**
**Visit www.mikerevell.com**